"Let's ditch Rias and the others!"

HIGH SCHOOL
DxD

7
RAGNAROK AFTER SCHOOL

RAGNAROK AFTER SCHOOL

7

ICHIEI ISHIBUMI

ILLUSTRATION BY
MIYAMA-ZERO

YEN
ON

New York

Volume 7
Ichiei Ishibumi

Translation by Haydn Trowell
Cover art by Miyama-Zero

This book is a work of fiction. Names, characters, places, and incidents are the product of the author's imagination or are used fictitiously. Any resemblance to actual events, locales, or persons, living or dead, is coincidental.

HIGH SCHOOL DXD Vol. 7 HOUKAGO NO RAGNAROK
©Ichiei Ishibumi, Miyama-Zero 2010
First published in Japan in 2010 by KADOKAWA CORPORATION, Tokyo.
English translation rights arranged with KADOKAWA CORPORATION, Tokyo, through TUTTLE-MORI AGENCY, INC., Tokyo.

English translation © 2022 by Yen Press, LLC

Yen On
150 West 30th Street, 19th Floor
New York, NY 10001

Visit us at yenpress.com
facebook.com/yenpress
twitter.com/yenpress
yenpress.tumblr.com
instagram.com/yenpress

First Yen On Edition: April 2022

Yen On is an imprint of Yen Press, LLC.
The Yen On name and logo are trademarks of Yen Press, LLC.

The publisher is not responsible for websites (or their content) that are not owned by the publisher.

Library of Congress Cataloging-in-Publication Data
Names: Ishibumi, Ichiei, 1981– author. | Miyama-Zero, illustrator. | Trowell, Haydn, translator.
Title: High school DxD / Ichiei Ishibumi ; illustration by Miyama-Zero ; translation by Haydn Trowell.
Other titles: Haisukūru Dī Dī. English
Description: First Yen On edition. | New York, NY : Yen On, 2020.
Identifiers: LCCN 2020032159 | ISBN 9781975312251 (v. 1 ; trade paperback) |
    ISBN 9781975312275 (v. 2 ; trade paperback) | ISBN 9781975312299 (v. 3 ; trade paperback) |
    ISBN 9781975312312 (v. 4 ; trade paperback) | ISBN 9781975312336 (v. 5 ; trade paperback) |
    ISBN 9781975312350 (v. 6 ; trade paperback) | ISBN 9781975312374 (v. 7 ; trade paperback)
Subjects: CYAC: Fantasy. | Demonology—Fiction. | Angels—Fiction. | High schools—Fiction. | Schools—Fiction.
Classification: LCC PZ7.1.I836 Hi 2020 | DDC [Fic]—dc23
LC record available at https://lccn.loc.gov/2020032159

ISBNs: 978-1-9753-1237-4 (paperback)
        978-1-9753-1238-1 (ebook)

10 9 8 7 6 5 4 3 2 1

LSC-C

Printed in the United States of America

CONTENTS

Your *peace* is excruciating for some people.

Life.0

"*Bwa-ha-ha-ha! It's time for you to meet your end, Breast Dragon Emperor!*"

An enemy dressed like a typical mysterious villain from an adventure movie broke out into laughter.

"*What?! The Breast Dragon Emperor will never be defeated by the likes of your army of darkness! Let's go! Balance Breaker!*"

With that, the superhero-like figure who looked just like me began a spectacular transformation sequence.

The end result matched my Balance Breaker armor perfectly.

We members of the Gremory Familia, along with Irina and Azazel, were having a TV night in the hall beneath my family home.

The show on-screen was a special effects spectacular titled *The Breast Dragon Emperor*. Supposedly, it was getting rave reviews in the underworld.

As you may have guessed from the title…I was the main character!

That said, I wasn't playing myself in the role. Using CGI, my face had been superimposed on top of an actor around the same height as me.

"…I heard it was an instant hit. You're a superhero now, Breast Dragon Emperor," Koneko remarked dryly from her spot on my lap, her tail swinging from side to side. She sure knew a lot about the goings-on in the underworld.

I, too, had already heard that it had become an instant hit. Viewer ratings had apparently hit over 50 percent with the very first episode. Admittedly, the program's success was rather startling. To think that anyone would make a TV show based on me, and then for it to become so popular down in the underworld...

The story went like this:

Issei "Gremory" is a young, up-and-coming demon who made a pact with a legendary dragon. He transforms to fight against an evil organization intent on destroying demonkind.

That Issei is utterly in love with breasts and fights to protect them. And to defeat these evildoers, he becomes the legendary Breast Dragon! Or so I gathered from watching it.

The watch party was my first time actually seeing the show in person, and as happy as I was to bask in my newfound fame, I was also kind of embarrassed!

The House of Gremory owned the copyright to the work, and *The Breast Dragon Emperor* was making them a considerable profit... Merchandise and licensing fees and whatnot... Demons sure knew how to move fast when they spotted a business opportunity, huh?

They had even sent me a prototype version of a Boosted Gear toy. It was incredible, albeit a bit creepy, how close it was to the real thing. It even played a bunch of catchphrases from an embedded speaker.

"The way they've recreated the Boosted Gear's Scale Mail is amazing. It looks just like the actual thing." Kiba nodded as he munched on his popcorn.

Even I had to admit that the studio had reproduced my armor incredibly faithfully.

"*Let's go, evildoers! Take this! Dragon Kick!*"

The armor-clad Breast Dragon performed a flashy special technique against the mystery villains, engulfing them in an explosion.

However, the protagonist found himself in hot water only a moment later, when the enemy leveled their latest weapon at him. Yet when all seemed lost, the heroine appeared.

"Breast Dragon! I'm here!"

A young woman garbed in a dress entered the scene—the prez! Of course, it wasn't the real prez, just an actress with a similar build whose face had been digitally altered to resemble Rias.

"Ah! Switch Princess! Nothing can hold us back now!"

With that, the Breast Dragon touched the Switch Princess's chest!

Whoa! Hold on! Why's it having such an effect on him?! And what's with that name, Switch Princess?! Isn't that what Bikou called her?! Is that her official title now or something?!

After touching those so-called switches, the Breast Dragon's body began to glow red as his power returned to him.

"The Breast Dragon and the Switch Princess are the good guys. Whenever they're in trouble, the Breast Dragon can touch the Switch Princess's knockers to turn invincible," Azazel explained with an amused tone.

Slap! The prez hit him over the head with a paper fan.

"...Grayfia told me everything, Azazel. Th-this whole 'Switch Princess' thing was *your* idea. You're the one who suggested it to the production team, weren't you? It's your fault I've been put in this... situation." The prez's face turned bright red. She looked to be biting back a fit of anger.

"What's the problem? From what I've heard, you've now got yourself a pretty big following among younger demographics. If anything, you're even more popular than you were before," Azazel replied, rubbing the back of his head where Rias had struck him.

I had caught wind that a magazine that was originally going to run a "Rias Gremory Special Edition" was now going with a "Let's All Be Switch Princesses!" special.

"...I'll never be able to show my face outside again," the prez muttered.

She had a point. I was skittish to walk the streets of the underworld now, too. Kids would probably point at me and shout, *Hey! It's the Breast Dragon!*

"*What does it matter where we go? This broadcast ensures you and I will forever be known as the Breast Dragon Emperor...*"

Ddraig, the legendary dragon who dwelled inside me, had been feeling particularly down lately. He let out a regretful sigh.

Sorry, Ddraig. Still, it seems to me like you're enjoying this to some degree.

"*Yeah, there's never a dull moment with you... Heh-heh-heh, I've got a lot to look forward to from here on out... Hahhhh...*"

And just like that, his enthusiasm was gone, and he looked depressed again.

I'll have to do something to cheer him up... Hold on, when did our positions switch? He'd always been the one to encourage me. *Get better soon, Red Dragon Emperor.*

"It's so amazing seeing my childhood friend become world-famous!" Irina exclaimed with her usual buoyant attitude. The young angel appeared to have really been enjoying this whole Breast Dragon thing.

Despite Irina now being a member of Heaven's forces, she had no trouble getting along with everyone else in the Occult Research Club. After all, she was technically a member, even if she didn't necessarily view it that way.

"You used to love superheroes when you were a kid, right, Issei? We always played make-believe games like this show, remember?" Irina asked, striking a dynamic pose.

Ah, she's right. I used to do that all the time.

"We sure did. You were so boyish back then. And now look how beautiful you are. I suppose there's no predicting how people are going to end up," I said.

Irina's face instantly blushed at these words. "Oh dear! Issei, don't try to seduce me like that! I-is this how you charmed Rias and the others...? How terrifying! You'll make me fall from Heaven! I'll become a fallen angel!"

Whoa! Her wings are flashing between white and black! Is she about to fall now?

Apparently, when an angel gave in to temptation or greed, or allowed a demon to seduce them, this was what happened.

Watching from the sidelines, Azazel let out a hearty laugh. "Ha-ha-ha, don't worry. We'll welcome you into our ranks with open arms, servant of Michael. The fallen angels already have a VIP seat lined up for you."

"Nooooo! The boss of the fallen angels is trying to recruit me! Archangel Michael, save meeeee!" Irina put her hands together in prayer, tears welling up in the corners of her eyes.

"I'm so proud of you, Issei. You're famous now."

"Yeah, me too. This is good publicity for our Familia, right?"

From beside me, both Asia and Xenovia flashed me warm smiles.

Strange though it was, I couldn't deny that this Breast Dragon thing was a success. It had all come as a bit of a shock, and I *was* embarrassed about it, but I didn't dislike it. Heck, I was grateful. This fame could be one more step on my journey toward earning myself a higher status in demon society. It might even aid me in becoming popular with the ladies of the underworld!

Hmm... The next time I walk the streets of the underworld, I may be accosted by a swarm of beautiful girls! Some of them might even come back with me to a hotel! That would be a dream come true...

Something soft pressed against my back, pulling me back to reality. *Plop.*

I knew this feeling! This wonderful sense of pliable elasticity! Looking back, I spied Akeno staring at me.

She rested her head on my shoulder and whispered into my ear with her stimulating, sensual voice, "I don't mind you seducing Irina, but isn't it about time you kept your promise with me?"

She pressed her cheek against mine! Electricity coursed through my skin! Her silky smooth face! Was there anything better?!

Asia looked on with displeasure from beside me. The prez's eyes twitched. Koneko, still sitting on my lap, silently pinched my thigh.

Ow, that hurt, Koneko...

"Promise?" I repeated back to Akeno, despite the disapproval of the others.

"To go on a date with me," Akeno responded with a bright-eyed smile. "That's what you said during our battle against Diodora Astaroth."

"Ah, I suppose I did. You remembered."

I *had* offered something like that to Akeno, but only because Koneko had told me to. Did that mean I really had to go through with it?

"Why would I forget? Don't tell me you were lying, Issei...?"

Ah, that's not fair, Akeno! Don't make such a dejected face. I'm helpless against those eyes!

"I-it wasn't a lie!"

Honestly, there was no reason to turn her down. Heck, a date with Akeno would be amazing!

I had tried to answer casually, but the person in question caught me in a tight hug, her voice truly ecstatic. "I'm so happy. How about our next day off, then, Issei? Heh-heh, my first date with Issei!" she all but sang.

A date with Akeno, huh?

That certainly sounded enjoyable, but the other girls were glaring at us...

Life.1
Nothing Beats Peace

It was time for our daily lunch break at Kuou Academy. I was eating together with Matsuda, Motohama, and Asia.

"The school trip is coming up quick. We need to decide on our group," Motohama stated as he picked at his rolled omelet.

We second-year students were supposed to be going to Kyoto for a few days. With everything else that had been going on, I had forgotten all about it. The second-year school trip came pretty soon after the Sports Festival.

It was supposed to be around the period that we changed to our winter uniforms. That said, there would probably still be some lingering summer heat.

"Um, the groups are of three or four, right?" I asked.

Matsuda nodded. "Yep. That's how many each room at the place we'll be staying at can hold. I guess we'll bunk together, right? We're the least popular guys in class, after all."

As if that needed saying. I was already painfully aware of that fact.

After the life-and-death struggle I had gone through during summer vacation, my reputation seemed to have improved a little—but that didn't change the fact that all the girls at school still thought of us three as the Perverted Trio. There were more girls at Kuou Academy than boys, so once our reputations had been established, they were incredibly hard to break free from.

At least I had friends in Asia, Xenovia, Irina, and Kiryuu, though. We even ate lunch together regularly. Every other girl avoided me like the plague, however.

"Hey, Perverted Trio. If you think you can handle four beauties, how about you pair with our group during the trip?" proposed the glasses-wearing Kiryuu with an especially lecherous grin.

Saying handle *like that totally gives me the creeps!*

"Hmm, teaming up with the Beauty Trio… That's excluding you, of course." Matsuda bobbed his head in thought, and Kiryuu slapped it from behind.

"Shut up or we'll exclude *you*. So how about it? What do you say, Hyoudou? You're not gonna turn down Asia, right?"

"Won't you join us, Issei?" Asia pleaded with a sweet smile.

Umph! There's no way I could refuse when she asked like that!

"Of course. I'm definitely okay with it!"

"Yes!"

Asia and I forgot all about our lunches, embracing each other in a wide-armed hug!

"Y-you both look like you've become a lot *closer* since the Sports Festival… When you aren't talking about each other, you keep staring all lovey-dovey," Kiryuu remarked as she adjusted her glasses.

"Heh-heh-heh. Asia and I are one in body and mind! We're always together. Right?"

With that, I opened my mouth to let Asia feed me a piece of sausage.

"Yes. I'll always stay by your side, Issei."

Recent events had undeniably brought Asia and me closer together. Before, I had thought of us as something akin to brother and sister and had always tried to protect her as an older sibling would've, but now…

Well, after that kiss, I'd been feeling strangely aware of Asia. Rather than a sister, I had started thinking of her as a girl I was close to. Consequently, she felt even more precious to me.

I had always treasured Asia and thought of her as lovely, but after rescuing her from Diodora, I'd realized she was an irreplaceable part of my life.

I want to be with her forever! I had thought to myself resolutely. Not as a lover, but as a family member of the opposite sex. No longer a younger sister.

Asia and I would stick together until one of us passed away. I was sure of it. Whether that would be hundreds or thousands of years from now, I didn't know, but I would treasure Asia for all of my days.

Oh, and we had one other secret.

Since that whole affair with Diodora, Asia greeted me with a kiss on the cheek every morning!

"Well, seeing as that's how it is, we'll team up with you guys. Asia is too purehearted to leave with anyone else. She wouldn't be able to turn down someone's advances. You'll keep her safe, though, right, Hyoudou? This way, Xenovia and Irina won't have to worry about her, either."

Xenovia paused between bits of her unusually large lunch, nodding. "Yeah, I'm good joining Issei, too."

"It will be more fun with him!" Irina agreed with a bread roll in hand.

"Damn yooooouuuuu! Why does Issei have to be so popular?! Ah, why are you so cruel, God?! *I want a beauty like Asia to hug meeeee!*" Matsuda wailed at the top of his voice.

Ah, God is dead, buddy. It's merciless, I know. And besides, I'm not popular per se. I've just been placed in an environment where it kind of looks that way from the outside.

There was no telling my friend all that, unfortunately. From his perspective, I probably did seem to be exceptionally blessed.

Hold on, if we're just talking about Asia, then maybe I am? I mean, my love for her is different from the kind of affection I picture in a harem. It's...more complicated than that, maybe?

"Hmm. It kind of looks to me like only Issei has been tagged for success... If I could find those tags, I would smash every last one of them with a hammer...," Motohama muttered under his breath as he straightened his glasses the same way Kiryuu had. It very nearly sounded like he was trying to curse me.

You're scaring me there, buddy...

"All right, then! We'll form a group of seven. Kiyomizu-dera, here we come! Kinkaku-ji and Ginkaku-ji, too!" Kiryuu declared with a twinkle in her glasses.

With that, our team was assembled. Three guys—me, Matsuda, and Motohama—and four girls—Asia, Xenovia, Irina, and Kiryuu. We would all be touring Kyoto together.

Next, we would have to decide where we wanted to go in the city and inform our teacher. There was supposed to be a place called Tenryuu-ji, the Temple of the Heavenly Dragon, in Kyoto, right? Seeing as one of the Two Heavenly Dragons resided inside me, checking out the place felt like a good idea.

Our school trip was right around the corner.

Hmm... In that case, perhaps I should invite Asia and the others to go shopping so we can pick up whatever we might need beforehand?

Classes had ended, and we were in the clubroom, talking about the upcoming trip over cups of tea. It was almost time to go home.

Our official club adviser, Azazel, hadn't come in to see us today. Lately, he'd been going back and forth to the underworld to discuss something. Bigwigs sure had it rough. He still made an effort to show up at school when necessary, however, so he must have been enjoying life here.

"Say, isn't the second-year school trip coming up?" the prez asked as she took a sip from her cup.

"Where did you and Akeno go last year?" I asked her.

"We went to Kyoto, too," Akeno replied. "We made the rounds at Kinkaku-ji, Ginkaku-ji, and the other famous sites."

The prez nodded. "Yes. But there are only so many places you can visit in three days and four nights. You should work out where you want to go ahead of time and plan everything out down to the hour. Make sure you factor in time for meals, too, or you'll regret it. You'll probably be taking the subway or the bus mainly, but you can still lose a lot of time moving from place to place."

"We made a big mistake by not properly understanding how long it would take to move around the city. The president wanted to see everything, but in the end, we didn't have enough time to visit our last stop, Nijo Castle. The president was fuming all the way home," Akeno explained with a faint smile.

The prez blushed. "I thought you said you wouldn't tell anyone that! I was in such high spirits. I love Japan, so it had always been my dream to visit Kyoto. Perhaps I obsessed over the streets and souvenirs a little more than I should have." Rias seemed wistful as she recounted the experience. She must have really enjoyed herself.

"Had you never been to Kyoto before? Couldn't you just use a magic circle to jump there whenever you want?" I asked.

The prez wagged her finger. "You don't understand, Issei. It's different going there for the first time on a school trip. Using a magic circle? I wouldn't do anything as vulgar as that. I had been dying to visit that ancient city for years. It wouldn't have been the same had I not explored it on my own two feet. I needed to feel the atmosphere on my skin."

The prez's eyes were positively sparkling. She really did become all whimsical when she spoke about the Japan of her dreams.

I recalled her saying once that, even after inheriting her position as the next head of the House of Gremory, she still wanted to spend her days going back and forth between Japan and the underworld.

Azazel had said something about joining us on the trip, too. Apparently, he was also eagerly anticipating being in Kyoto.

Having finished her tea, Rias changed the subject. "Your trip is important, but we also need to think about what we're going to do for the Academy Festival."

"Oh yeah, that's coming up soon, too, right? The Sports Festival, the school trip, and the Academy Festival all take place right after one another... It's going to be hard for us second-years..."

The calendar for the second semester was filled with special events.

Akeno handed the prez a sheet of paper. It looked like we were expected to write a proposal for the Occult Research Club's activity plan for submission to the student council.

"We need to decide on something and start planning now. If we work out our plan before you all head to Kyoto, the rest of us can start preparing while you're away. It's a good thing we have so many members this year."

The prez was right, of course. The school trip was important, but we couldn't afford to forget about the Academy Festival, either!

"I'm looking forward to all the activities!" Asia seemed to be overjoyed. She loved these kinds of things.

Although her expression remained calm, Xenovia's eyes shone as she added, "Yeah. I'm a big fan of these high school functions, too. The Sports Festival was fantastic."

She had gone on a bit of a rampage during the Sports Festival, dominating one event after another. By the time she was finished, every girls' sports club at school was trying to poach her from the Occult Research Club.

"I've never done anything like this before, but I'm excited! I transferred here at the perfect time! Surely, this must be Archangel Michael's providence," Irina proclaimed, offering a prayer to the heavens.

Our Church Maiden Trio was definitely pumped about the Academy Festival. Maybe it was because they missed all the pageantry and tradition of the Church, and this felt similar?

"Last year...you did a haunted house, right? I wasn't a member of the Occult Research Club back then, but everyone was talking about it. I heard it was pretty realistic," I said.

I hadn't visited it myself, but one of my classmates had and later told us all how lifelike everything had been. The ghosts and monsters had apparently looked like the real thing.

"Yes, I'm sure it *was* scary. We did use real monsters, after all," the prez stated as if it were nothing.

"R-real monsters...?" I repeated in surprise.

"Yes," the prez affirmed with a relaxed smile. "I asked some creatures that weren't a threat to humans to aid with our haunted house. They were in need of work, too, so it was a win-win for all of us. We owe last year's success to them."

The prez and Akeno broke out into amused, sisterly chuckles.

"The student council was a little angry at us afterward. Sona was still vice president back then, but that didn't stop her from chewing us out. She claimed that using real creatures was unforgivable," Akeno recalled.

I had to agree with the chairwoman. It sounded like way more than just a simple violation.

"So are we doing a haunted house again this year? Or maybe we could hold a circus show? How about a vampire in a cardboard box?"

Gasper, his cheeks puffed up, began to hit me over the head at that last suggestion. "You're so mean, Isseeeeeiiiii! I'm always the butt of your jokes!"

Teasing one's underclassmen was a privilege of being an upperclassman! I planned to keep messing around with Gasper until the day I graduated. He was my precious underclassman, so I would take good care of him.

Despite my less than serious proposals, the prez made a pensive face. "Maybe we should try something new this time—"

Yet before she could finish speaking, our phones all began to ring at once.

We glanced at one another. Everyone knew what this meant.

Immediately, the prez's reaction shifted to one that was far sterner. "Let's go."

-O●O-

With Irina in tow, the rest of the Gremory Familia and I made our way to an abandoned factory on the other side of town.

The sun had already set, and the sky was getting dark. We could sense the presence of several individuals inside—along with an unmistakable feeling of hostility and murderous intent.

"So you're the Gremory Familia? You didn't waste any time getting here, I see."

A man clad in a black coat approached us out of the darkness. Various humanoid figures were lurking in the shadows around him, all watching us. There had to be at least a hundred of them.

The prez stepped forward, addressing the speaker in a cold tone of voice. "You're with the Khaos Brigade's Hero Faction, I presume? Greetings. I'm Rias Gremory, the high-class demon entrusted with watching over this town by the three great powers."

The man's lips curled in a smirk at this salutation. "Ah, I know who you are, sister of the Demon King. And we are here to purify this town of demons, to save it from *you.*" He glanced at each of us in turn, clearly regarding us as filth.

Yep, this guy belonged to the Khaos Brigade's so-called Hero Faction! Lately, these guys had caused several incidents throughout town, attacking important locations associated with the three great powers.

It was our job to take care of them. Most of the time, the perpetrators were human, but every now and then...

Two figures appeared on either side of the black-coat man, who was their apparent leader. These two, at least, were also human. One was concealing his eyes behind a pair of sunglasses, while the other was wearing traditional Chinese clothing. Like their boss, they were both males. Judging by their appearances, all three of them were foreigners, too.

None of the many other hostile beings in the factory were human. To put it simply, the strange bipedal figures were low-level creatures that served the Hero Faction, which used them for attacks like this.

Nonetheless, they rivaled mid-class demons in strength at the bare minimum. We couldn't match them in a direct fight.

My gauntlet let out a brilliant red flash. The countdown for my Balance Breaker's activation was complete! I summoned my armor and stepped forward to the front of our group. As I did so, I removed my Ascalon Holy Sword and threw it to Xenovia, who caught it in one hand.

Kiba and I formed the vanguard of our group, with Xenovia only a few paces behind us. Her role was to fight on the front lines while also providing support as needed.

Irina, Koneko, and Gasper stood in the middle of our formation. Their duty was to support those of us leading the charge while guarding the members at the back. Koneko and Irina in particular were to defeat any enemies who managed to make their way past the vanguard.

The rearguard was composed of the prez, Akeno, and Asia. Naturally, the prez issued the orders while simultaneously providing aid. Akeno's duty was attacking from long range with demonic magic, while Asia was responsible for healing any who got hurt.

Including Irina, this was the signature arrangement of the Occult Research Club—3-3-3. Without my Balance Breaker, I would be assigned a support role in the middle, changing the formation to 2-4-3.

This was an altogether different arrangement from what we used during our Rating Games. At such times, we had to decide how to move across the battlefield in smaller groups.

As our opponents watched us get into place, the man in the black coat summoned what looked like a ball of white flame in the palm of his hand.

I saw Kiba's eyes narrow. "—! So he's a Sacred Gear user, too..."

Ah. Another one.

The people whom the Hero Faction had sent after us almost all had Sacred Gears of their own. In other words, they were using the special powers bestowed on them by God's still-active Sacred Gear program to come after us.

"What a bother. We've been fighting Sacred Gear users one after another lately." The prez let out a resigned sigh, yet her eyes glowed with determination.

The man with his white ball of flame drew closer to us. Yet before he could do anything...

Boom!

...I activated the propulsion engine on my back, shooting straight for him and blowing away his attack!

Boooooooooooom!

Our opponents dodged the deflected mass of energy, but I had succeeded in eliminating at least ten of their subordinate combatants.

Once defeated, those creatures simply evaporated into thin air.

Dammit! I thought. The building was cramped, limiting my movements. With the intensity of my power output, I could end up destroying a lot more than just this old factory.

What's more, the fact that the black-coat man had been able to dodge my charge meant he was a well-trained fighter himself! Even so, it was clear our side possessed the upper hand.

At that moment, one of the creatures fighting for the Hero Faction exclaimed, "Watch out for the Red Dragon Emperor! A single attack from him could kill any one of us! But his movements will be limited inside the factory!"

They'd caught on.

I assembled some demonic energy into my hand, holding back as best I could, and hurled it toward the front of the building.

Boom!

A miniaturized Dragon Shot! Against any human opponent, it would have been enough to settle the fight! After my battle against Saji, I had spent a good deal of effort training for small-scale combat. It had turned out to be surprisingly useful for encounters around town.

I had already eliminated several members of the Hero Faction this way during previous attacks on our territory.

Typically, blasts like that one were enough to eliminate a target in one blow.

Pshhhhh!

This time, however, my Dragon Shot disappeared! Just as it had been about to connect with its target, the shadows surrounding us seemed to extend and swallow the attack.

Hold on, is that what actually happened? Does one of these people have the ability to control darkness?

It was the man with the sunglasses. His Sacred Gear...

Swoosh!

Kiba lunged forward with incredible speed. He brought his Holy Demon Sword down on the sunglasses-wearing man. Unfortunately, the shadows surrounding him moved quicker, engulfing Kiba's blade in a fraction of a second!

Whoosh!

The Holy Demon Sword emerged from the mass of darkness, plunging back toward its owner! Kiba swung around to dodge it, then stepped backward.

"So you can transfer what enters one shadow into another... An indirect attacking style that parries oncoming attacks. What a pain," Kiba remarked with a scowl.

Now I understood what was happening. One shadow swallowed an attack, and then another released it from a different direction.

Er, wait, what about that miniaturized Dragon Shot?!

Vrrrrrnnnnnn!

I could feel the air vibrating as my energy emerged from the darkness in one corner of the building. Sure enough, a red sphere of power was flying straight for Asia!

Xenovia had sensed the danger to Asia as well, but she was busy taking care of a large group of opponents.

"Don't you even dare!"

I quickly gathered another mass of energy, hurling it at the Dragon Shot veering toward Asia to destroy it!

Kra-boom!

The two projectiles collided with a violent explosion that coursed through the derelict building.

"Don't you lay a finger on Asia!" Xenovia cried out, shielding her.

Thanks, Xenovia!

She acted incredibly swiftly whenever Asia was in danger. We had all agreed to work together to help defend our blond beauty. Not just because Asia didn't have much in the way of combat abilities, but rather, as our healer, she was an essential member of our team. We couldn't afford to lose her in a fight.

Whenever she was in danger, the person best able to respond as quickly as possible would rush to her aid. On this occasion, that had been Xenovia.

Whoooooooooosh!

A blue glint from behind the blast caught my attention.

It was the man in the Chinese outfit, wielding a bow and arrow formed of concentrated light.

This was bad! Light was poison to us demons! And we were dealing with a foreign Sacred Gear! There was no telling what kind of special abilities that weapon might possess! Sure, *I* had my Red Dragon Emperor Scale Mail to protect me, but if any of the others sustained a direct hit, they would be in critical condition!

A luminous arrow lanced forward, and then it changed direction in midair! It could change trajectory even after release!

Fwp! Fwp!

A different shot of concentrated light came flying overhead from behind.

The two projectiles collided in midair, destroying each other in a brilliant flare.

"Leave light-based attacks to me!"

Glancing back, I saw Irina. As a reincarnated angel, she was capable of wielding holy light. She must have hurled a spear to counter our opponent.

Crack! Swoosh!

That was the sound of something freezing over and of cutting wind! Akeno had hurled a volley of ice spears generated with her demonic magic at the man in the Chinese outfit.

Again, the shadows ballooned and consumed them before they could reach their target, casting them instead toward the prez. Rias dodged them as if they were nothing, however. She sure was amazing!

Suddenly, the shadows gathered around the bowman in Chinese attire, forming a wall of pitch darkness. A moment later, arrows began to shower down from all over. Balls of fire, too!

"Wha—?!"

I scrambled to brush away the attacks... Could our enemies still take aim even in the dark? As best I could tell, they had vanished entirely.

"Gasper! Do you have the data?" Kiba asked, turning his head in the direction of our resident vampire.

Gasper, who had been using a special device since the beginning of the fight, squealed back, "Yessssss! H-here! Th-that fire-type Sacred Gear is called the Flame Shake! And the shadow counter is called Night Reflection! The light-based offensive one is the Sterling Blue!"

Gasper had been busy using a device Azazel had given him to analyze our opponents' Sacred Gears. The scanning machine had proven exceptionally useful lately. It was super effective in fights against Sacred Gear users. So far, there hadn't been a single one that it had been unable to scan.

"Gasper! Once you're finished, drink my blood!" I called.

"O-okay!"

I had instructed him to carry a small vial filled with my blood on him at all times so that he could activate his own Sacred Gear and freeze his targets whenever necessary.

When Gasper fought in urban settings, he usually turned into a swarm of bats to survey the battlefield and locate where opponents were hiding. Koneko could use her sage magic to search for the *qi* energy of enemies and similarly determine their whereabouts. As such, our two first-years were the scouts.

Gasper's eyes were indeed powerful, but countless things could keep him from using them effectively in a battle between Sacred Gear users.

It looked like our present adversaries knew about his abilities, as whenever he tried to catch one of the three in his sights, they would shield themselves with one of their many disposable fighters to stop him from freezing them.

On top of that, they were clearly aware of our powers and had targeted our healer, Asia. Even the use of light-based weapons suggested these Hero Faction guys had been expecting demons.

"I guess the stronger you are, the more people will want to capture you for study," Kiba stated with a cynical grin.

Capture...? S-study...? At that moment, I remembered something Sairaorg had said to us.

"No matter how powerful you may be, if you keep repeating the same old tricks, you're bound to lose. Your opponents will take full advantage of any openings."

Openings, huh? We might have had an overwhelming advantage over our opponents in terms of raw ability, but they knew our techniques—our weaknesses.

First and foremost, those light-based attacks were a problem. We were demons, after all. If any of the others were to take a hit, they would be in trouble.

Kiba must have thought the same, as he had turned his gaze to the enemy bowman, who was still concealed behind that defensive shadow barrier. Fighters poured out in front of the Sacred Gear users. From the looks of it, they still had a considerable number of grunts left.

How were we going to get rid of that massive shadow? The best option was undoubtedly taking down the one controlling it, but he was obviously going to use the darkness to protect himself.

Given the situation, transferring my power to any of the others would also require careful consideration. Every single member of this Familia was already particularly strong, so lending them my boosted strength could wreak havoc. It was too great a risk while we were still in town. If we could go all out, there'd be no stopping us.

Ugh, I'm really not suited to all this tactical crap.

I was a Pawn, and my job was to hold the front line. I would just have to follow the prez's orders!

Sure enough, the command came less than a moment later. "Issei, your target is their flame user. Yuuto, their shadow user. Xenovia, your task is to take care of the grunts to open paths for the other two. The center and the rear will support the vanguard with everything they have! We'll annihilate every last one of those fighters!"

"Got it!" we responded in unison, setting to action!

Xenovia dashed ahead, dispersing the grunts with a single swing of the Ascalon!

That was a Power-type fighter for you! Her destructive potential was on a whole other level compared to regular combatants!

With the cannon fodder out of the way, Kiba and I set our sights on our targets!

Kiba closed in at incredible speed, carving through the wall of shadow enveloping the bowman!

Whoosh!

That was the sound of Kiba's Holy Demon Swords being sucked into the dark! No sooner had they vanished than they came flying out from elsewhere!

Swoosh!

One of them shot out from a shadow close to my target, their flame wielder!

"Issei! Dodge that thing and hit that shadow with your Dragon Shot!" the prez abruptly ordered. I didn't really follow the reasoning behind it, but I would do as instructed!

I moved out of the path of the oncoming Holy Demon Sword.

Ha! Thanks to all my sparring training with Kiba, I know how to handle this!

At the same moment, I unleashed a mass of red demon energy into the shadow!

Whoosh!

Whoa! My Dragon Shot got sucked right in again! Now I understood. The passage hadn't been closed yet!

"Yuuto! Your positions are connected through the shadow! Cut Issei's Dragon Shot in half before it exits! Detonate it!"

"Understood!"

Kiba did precisely as the prez commanded, plunging his Holy Demon Sword into the dark mass!

Boooooooooom!

"Augh!"

There was a powerful explosion, followed by a scream! The shadow user looked like he had been caught up in the blast, his outfit in tatters as he was thrown backward!

"I wanted to see what would happen if an attack burst inside that shadow. It seems our opponent couldn't redirect it all and ended up taking the brunt of the damage himself. Even if he can alter the trajectory of an attack, I'm guessing he can't change its full force," the prez declared with an indomitable grin.

How forward-thinking of her! That much was to be expected of our King!

As I looked at her in admiration, a glowing arrow came flying my way. This one was green instead of blue!

"—?!"

I was caught off guard by the sudden attack. Fortunately, I managed to dodge it, but no sooner had I done so than another came flying from a direction that appeared empty! The others were equally shocked by this new development.

The prez turned her gaze toward the factory. "It looks like we have another one to deal with. They must be attacking from a position of safety, using the darkness to redirect their shots. Perhaps that shadow power outlasts its user…"

What?! So there are others waiting to ambush us?! Do they seriously have two light users? To think they were trying to snipe us from a distance using that shadow ability. That thing sure was useful!

Ah, wait... It looked like it soon wore off after its wielder was defeated.

Gasper, who was still staring at the screen of his scanning device, suddenly cried out, "A-amazing! Th-the data has just come in! That last attack came from the Sterling Green!"

"I'll take care of that one, then. Koneko, you're with me. You can find the shooter via their *qi*, right?"

"...Yes, Xenovia."

Xenovia and Koneko, the latter with her ears standing up in full-on *nekomata* mode, made to leave the factory!

Oh right. I still have my own job to finish!

Vrnnnnnnnnnnnnnn!

Activating my propulsion unit, I shot forward!

"Damn you, Red Dragon Emperor! Burn in hell!"

The enemy flame user had gathered a tremendous mass of fire in his cupped hands, aiming it straight for me!

Vrnnnnnnnnnnnn!

It came racing my way but proved rather weak. Slightly warm at best. Maybe a little cool.

Riser Phenex's flames had felt scorching even through my armor. And compared to Tannin's fire breath, this was like a matchstick.

"If you want to burn me, bring a phoenix or a dragon next time!"

Thump!

My fist pushed straight through the flames, slamming deep into the man's gut. A direct hit.

And just as I brought that flame user down, Kiba finished taking care of the light user.

All the enemy Sacred Gear users were defeated. Or so I thought.

"...Nghahhhhhhhh!"

The shadow user, whom we had all thought was beaten, rose back to his feet, letting out a shrill cry.

A black haze wrapped around his body before spreading farther, stretching out to envelop the whole factory.

What is this chill creeping down my spine...? I could sense a strange power in that darkness, as if something had undergone a sudden change...

Flash!

A burst of light erupted under the shadow wielder's feet as a magic circle took shape. I had never seen its design before.

It looked like a teleportation array, but it clearly wasn't a demon one. It had none of the usual design features or symbols.

A fallen angel one, maybe? I thought. Even if it was, I still didn't recognize it. I had seen Azazel use magic circles countless times before, so I knew what to expect from them.

This one shone in a different way.

It closed in around the shadow user, and with a momentary flash, both it and our opponent vanished.

"Phew. It's over."

With the battle finished, I released my armor and stopped to catch my breath.

"Good work, Issei."

I wasn't injured, but Asia wrapped me in her healing aura regardless. It was wonderfully warm. The kindness alone was enough to leave me feeling refreshed.

The Hero Faction's many minions were scattered to the wind. Those still standing had fled the moment the shadow wielder had disappeared.

"Go to sleep now. Go to sleep now." Gasper was moving his fingers in a circular gesture, lulling the captured Sacred Gear users into unconsciousness. That was one of his vampire powers.

You look adorable doing that, Gaspy.

The prez and Akeno had opened a magic circle to send the captured pair off to the underworld.

All that was left was for Xenovia and Koneko to—

"It's done. We roughed him up a good bit, but we didn't kill him," Xenovia said, carrying the figure of an unconscious man over her shoulder.

Koneko was following along behind her.

Whoa, they beat him already? Way to go, you two!

Gasper worked his hypnotism on this final captive before the others threw him into the magic circle with his allies. It was a shame their coconspirator had managed to get away.

"Officials in the underworld can handle them now. Unfortunately, I don't think we'll be getting any useful information from them," the prez stated with a sigh.

We had sent other Sacred Gear-wielding captives from the Hero Faction to the underworld previously, but somehow, all memory of their involvement with the group was erased by the time of their arrest. We still had to send this new batch just to be sure, but our chances seemed low.

It appeared that the Hero Faction used some sort of memory adjustment programming whenever it sent operatives to attack one of the three great powers, erasing their memories in the event that they were captured. From what I'd heard, it was almost impossible to restore those memories once they were wiped.

I preferred sending them on to the underworld while still alive. It certainly beat the old principle of killing terrorists without exception.

Speaking of unusual situations, after my battle with Diodora, my own Sacred Gear had undergone a bit of an evolution.

The main transformation was to my Balance Breaker. Whereas it used to take me a hundred and twenty seconds to activate it before, I could now do so in thirty.

On top of that, the length of time that I could maintain it had improved considerably, up to two hours a day. According to Ddraig, if I was in a good physical and mental state when I did it, I might even be able to pull off three hours.

I could also trigger my Balance Breaker multiple times a day, too. So long as the total never exceeded two hours, I could activate it as much as I liked.

As such, its two major shortcomings had been improved considerably. It was an incredible step forward. Seriously, I was overpowered now... And this was all because of that Juggernaut Drive phenomenon.

That didn't mean I had nothing to worry about, though. I still hadn't caught up to Vali.

"You know, it isn't easy for us, a super-powered offensive team, to fight when worrying about collateral damage," I said to Kiba.

He flashed me a bitter smile. "It can't be helped. With our abilities, if we didn't hold back, we would end up destroying the whole town."

That was undoubtedly true. There were people in nearby homes and buildings, so destroying them was out of the question. Even if we were in an abandoned area, causing too much damage would risk alerting the townspeople to what was going on.

"If we think of this as another supplementary rule for the Rating Game, it's all good practice. We've already had to fight under similar conditions once before, after all."

The prez was right about that. The more Rating Games we played in the future, the more we would need to find ways of dealing with limiting rules. Adapting to such handicaps now would prove advantageous for surviving future battles.

To be honest, I had to admit that the experience we had gained fighting the Sitri Familia had helped us grow. I could regulate the powers of the Red Dragon Emperor to a decent degree now.

"They are wising up," Kiba muttered with a sigh.

"What do you mean?" I questioned.

"Some of these assassin Sacred Gear users have special skills. A fair number of them possess Support- and Technique-type abilities that are especially effective against demons. At first, they were all Power- and Wizard-types, remember...? I wonder if they're adjusting their strategy?"

Come to think of it, it felt like each time we engaged members of the Hero Faction, our battles were stretching longer and longer.

We had won every fight, of course, but there was no denying that our opponents were developing a firmer grasp of our combat style. Their assaults had been monotonous and straightforward at first, but they had gradually started to employ abilities we weren't familiar with... The shadow-type Sacred Gear they had sent this time was one such example.

"...Azazel did say there are a lot of unknowns when it comes to Sacred Gears," Koneko remarked.

The prez nodded in agreement. "Yes. That would explain why they tried to absorb and deflect the Red Dragon Emperor's powers and Kiba's Holy Demon Swords. They must have realized that if they can't block our attacks outright, there are still other ways they can defend themselves."

"U-um, there's something I'm a little unsure about... Do you mind?" Irina asked, timidly raising her hand.

"Please, go ahead," the prez urged her.

"It seems to me that this Hero Faction is acting pretty strangely if they're attacking just to gather intel on us."

"Strangely?" Xenovia repeated.

Irina nodded. "I mean, if they really wanted to defeat or capture us, they should be able to use the data from two or three encounters to put together an effective plan to strike us for real the fourth time, right? But they've hardly changed, even after the fifth battle. At first, I thought they were just acting overly cautious, but now... I wonder if their leaders are up to some kind of weird experiment."

"On us?" Akeno inquired.

Irina tilted her head to one side. "More like testing their Sacred Gear users, maybe... It's just a feeling, so I can't say anything for sure... The Hero Faction has sent forces to other places under the dominion of the three great powers. Maybe they're simply looking to duke it out with strong people?"

We all fell silent at this possibility.

I let out a groan of consternation at Irina's fresh opinion. Her theory did make sense. I had assumed the Hero Faction was simply trying to eliminate influential members of the three great powers.

Yet if they had some other reason for sending Sacred Gear users into battle against us...

"...A dramatic transformation," Koneko murmured.

Our expressions all stiffened.

I-it couldn't be!

"...Don't tell me...," I whispered, my voice dismayed. "They're sending all these people out to try to push one of them into Balance Breaker mode?"

"Issei. Remember how that shadow user acted just before disappearing into the magic circle... Doesn't it seem like that's what it was?" Kiba asked. I failed to find any evidence to deny it.

There had been an odd atmosphere about that shadow user. It certainly had looked like he had gotten his hands on something new, something different.

But was it really a Balance Breaker?

"Is fighting us enough for them to reach that level?" I wondered aloud.

The prez narrowed her eyes in thought. "...The Red Dragon Emperor, a wielder of Holy Lightning, one fighter with Holy Demon Swords, another with Durendal and Ascalon, a time-freezing vampire, a *nekomata* gifted in sage magic, and an exceptional healer... Issei, from our opponents' standpoints, we're a force to be reckoned with. Regardless of whether they win or lose, battling us must make for an extraordinary combat experience for regular humans."

So they were farming us like rare boss encounters to rack up experience points?! I suppose that did make sense. I had needed a good deal of practice myself, first from training with Tannin, then from fighting a descendent of the legendary Sun Wukong and a *nekomata* skilled in sage magic.

Ultimately, it was the prez's breasts that had pushed me over the line. That last step was probably different for everyone.

"What a crude method," Kiba spat.

"I get the impression they don't mind throwing away dozens or even hundreds of their people so long as at least one can reach their Balance Breaker...," Irina said. "Then again, watching their comrades fall in battle one by one might also help push them toward a dramatic change... Either way, it's so dreadful."

The prez shrugged. "There are still a lot of things we don't understand about the situation. I'll ask Azazel about it when I see him next. He might be able to offer a different perspective on all this."

We wouldn't be able to solve the mystery now, so we decided it was best to return to base. We activated our own magic circles and made our way back to the clubroom.

There we all took a bit of a break to catch our breath. Akeno began to hum a happy tune as we prepared to go home.

"Well now, Akeno. You look pleased. Did the fight help satisfy your sadist desires?" the prez asked.

Akeno responded with a broad smile. "No, that isn't it. Oh-ho-ho. I can't help but smile. Tomorrow, I'm going on a date. Issei will officially be my boyfriend."

Right, tomorrow was the day of our date.

The air suddenly went cold. I could feel the murderous gazes of the women in the room fall upon me.

–O●O–

"...How is it?" Koneko asked me. Once we were home, she had come to my room in full *nekomata* mode, ears and all.

"Yeah. It feels good."

She was putting everything into using her sage magic on me.

Lately, Koneko had taken to using her sage magic to wash away the fatigue I accumulated on rough days. While Asia could heal any physical trauma, she couldn't restore my depleted energy.

Koneko, however, could massage my *qi* so that my stamina was replenished by the following day. Apparently, proper manipulation of one's internal energy was a way to improve the body's natural healing processes, the circulation of one's blood, and so forth. That was what she was pouring her efforts into doing for me.

It felt really warm and good having her focus her *qi* on me like this…

Koneko was wearing nothing more than a thin white piece of clothing. Apparently, Akeno had given Koneko the garment on the assumption that a pure and clean appearance would make it easier for her to manipulate *qi*. However, it was so thin that…I had no trouble feeling her feminine flesh.

Petite though Koneko's frame was, her body was so soft that I couldn't help considering her as a true woman… No, I knew I shouldn't! I couldn't think that way about my underclassman!

That soft touch kept sending waves of heated feelings through my own flesh. It was an incredibly relaxing sensation, as if I were taking a bath at just the right temperature.

At the same time, I could feel the inside of my body getting hot.

"…Just as they help alleviate your exhaustion, these sage magic healing techniques will be able to gradually restore the huge amount of energy you burned up in your Juggernaut Drive state," Koneko said to me with a soft smile.

She looked a little flushed—probably embarrassed because I, a man, was embracing her.

Just as she had explained to me, this pleasantness coursing through my body was the life force I had burned through being restored bit by bit.

"Yeah, I heard I shortened my life when I used my Juggernaut Drive."

"At this rate, you won't even live another hundred years."

That was what Azazel had told me after the Sports Festival. He'd spoken to Ddraig about the state of my body while I'd been unconscious.

Even if it wasn't my full Juggernaut Drive, being in that state had drastically shortened my life expectancy, to the point where I was unlikely to last another century. That one battle had eaten away most of my time in this world.

A hundred years might sound like plenty of time for a human, but it was incredibly short for a demon. When the prez found out...she wept. I couldn't stand to let Asia know about it. We had promised to stay by each other's sides. I'm sure she would have been distraught had she known.

The next time I entered that form, whether complete or not, I would die. After realizing as much, I could literally feel my face blanch in fear.

It had come as such a shock. Worst of all was that I would have to part ways with my friends, with the prez, with Asia, after no more than a hundred years. It was unbearably disheartening.

I guess it might sound weird for a teenager to worry about dying in a century's time, but if someone told you that you wouldn't live another hundred years when you were expecting to live ten thousand, you would be shocked, too.

I had only been a demon for around six months, and in that time, I had used up 99 percent of my days. *Shocked* didn't even begin to describe it. If I had whittled away at my life force bit by bit, I might have been able to stand it, but this time, I had expended the vast majority in one go.

There was no telling if a measly century was enough to get promoted and become a harem king.

The Dividing Gear was now off-limits. From the sound of it, I would die if I tried to use it in my present state. Absorbing any other abilities that conflicted with my own could also prove fatal.

There was no problem using my regular Red Dragon Emperor powers, but pushing beyond my limits would also risk eating away at my life span.

Vali seemed to be capable of drawing on his vast store of demonic power instead of trading away his life force. I, however, never had that much demonic power to begin with... The more I drew on power from the Heavenly Dragon within me that exceeded what I could handle, the closer I would move to death.

Letting anger carry me past those limits would spell the end...

However, Azazel had mentioned there was a way to restore my lost energy, although only at a fraction at a time.

The treatment used sage magic.

My Juggernaut Drive had eaten away at my existence, but so long as my core life energy wasn't destroyed or dried out, it could gradually be restored to its original state with sage magic.

"...A lot of people would be sad if you died, Issei... I would hate it, too. That's why I want to take the time to replenish what's been lost... Even if it takes me my whole life... So don't transform like that again...," Koneko entreated me with teary eyes.

My heart skipped a beat!

When you ask me like that, Koneko, I couldn't possibly say no!

"Yeah, I understand. I won't worry you all like that again. I mean, I'm not exactly confident about that, seeing as I can't even remember how it happened, but still, I'll do everything possible not to use that Juggernaut Drive again."

"...Thank you," Koneko whispered, hugging me tightly.

She was all but begging me never to do something that foolish again.

When I'd first met Koneko, I never would've expected that poison-tongued, overpowered petite girl to hold me in her arms like this... I was so happy! *Skinship* with Koneko was awesome!

Besides, I didn't want to kick the bucket before becoming a harem king. Or rather, I didn't want to die before having sex with the prez! Akeno, too! And I still needed to make a baby with Xenovia!

Lately, I even found myself wondering what it would be like to have that sort of relationship with Asia, too. I didn't want to pass away before fulfilling those dreams.

As I thought on the renewed meaning of my desires, Koneko's face flushed. "…Issei, there's a faster way."

"Huh? What do you mean?"

"…F-Fangzhongshu."

What was that? I had never heard that word before.

"Fang-zhong-shu? What's that?"

"…It's a technique that women skilled in manipulating *qi* can use to join their energy with a man and encourage his vitality."

"Hmm. I had no idea there was a technique that convenient. Maybe we could try that next time?"

At my proposal, Koneko's face reddened even further. She looked a little flustered, but she nodded, as if affirming her determination. "…I—I understand. I-it will be my first time, too…"

…*Huh? What's with that strange reaction?*

I wondered if I should try getting some details from Koneko. The last thing I needed right now was some kind of wacky misunderstanding.

"…Hey, by the way, how exactly do you do this *Fangzhongshu*?"

Koneko's voice trembled in embarrassment as she answered my question. "…Th-the man and the woman…have to become one… Th-that way, a woman sage magic user can send her energy directly into the man…"

—*! H-hey, hey, hey, hey, hey!*

"Th-that's…sex! Ngh!"

Koneko rushed to cover my mouth with both hands. "T-too loud, Issei." Only after I nodded did she pull her palms away.

I paused for a moment to take a deep breath before responding in a low voice, "B-but that would mean you and me… W-we can't!"

That was insane! I would never have imagined that *Fangzhongshu*, or whatever it was called, was actually sex…!

"A-am I not good enough…?"

Koneko was staring up at me with sorrowful eyes! Perhaps it was me, but she looked way sexier than usual!

"N-no, that's not it! I mean, you're my underclassman, and it's still..."

It was all too soon! Still, I swallowed my words. I knew at once that they would only upset her.

"I'm grateful, really. But if we aren't careful, you could end up getting pregnant... Ah, but you're a *youkai*, and I'm a demon who used to be human, so I guess maybe that's impossible, right?"

"No, when *nekomata* have children, it's usually with men from other races... Most of the time, they're human males."

Our conversation had suddenly shifted to how *nekomata* lived their lives, but that was fine. It was best we changed the topic. It kind of scared me that Koneko cared so deeply about her friends that she was willing to give up her virginity to help treat me! That was something she should only consider once she was in love!

"Aren't there any male *nekomata*?"

A safe question. Good work, me. Let's keep away from the issue of sex and keep talking about nekomata!

"...There aren't many, but they do exist... However, female *nekomata* prefer to follow the old traditions and take mates from other races."

So it was tradition, was it? I could believe that. Even for *youkai*, there had to be different customs among the varying species.

"...*Nekomata* are so few in number that I'll have to bear children of my own... I've been reborn as a demon, but I still want children..."

Koneko wanted kids in the future, just like Xenovia. When that time came, I would feel better if she did it with someone she genuinely loved.

I nodded as she explained her thoughts on the matter to me.

Then, somewhat hesitantly, Koneko glanced up at me, her eyes radiating both embarrassment and determination, and murmured softly, "...M-my body and breasts are still small... But I can still have s-s-sex... I—I can bear children... A-and if you're really in danger, Issei, I won't have any choice but to do *Fangzhongshu*... I—I'm ready..."

Bah!

Blood spurted from my nose with considerable force.

That erotic tone of voice sent my imagination whirling!

No! No, we can't, Koneko!

"K-Koneko! Th-that's…! You can't let yourself become sex-obsessed!"

"…B-but if I'm going to live with you all, I—I feel like I have to know about these things… Recently, I've even started to think that maybe…"

What on earth?! The prez and Akeno have poisoned her mind!

I placed my hands on Koneko's shoulders. This issue needed to be addressed seriously.

Please forgive my excessive nosebleeds! I can't help them, not when I hear such enthralling words come from the lips of a girl—even Koneko!

"Listen to me, Koneko! I've said this to Asia as well! You shouldn't try to compete with the prez and Akeno! You can't let yourself start picking up overly sexual traits from our Two Great Ladies or me! You need to stay as Koneko forever! I'm very strict about these things!"

It turned out that the prez's and Akeno's erotic attacks influenced more than just me. They were influencing the other club members, too! That wouldn't do! My Two Great Ladies, with their erotic bodies, were capable of terrible erotic assaults. If our purer members like Asia and Koneko were to end up that way…I would be at risk of losing all sense of reason!

"…But Asia is trying her hardest, too…" Koneko's tone of voice seemed a little disappointed.

Did I need to make another push? What was I doing? I was supposed to be going on a date with Akeno tomorrow!

"Koneko! You shouldn't imitate the prez or Akeno, all right? Th-they're bad role models!"

"Shouldn't imitate us? Tell me, what are you talking about in here?"

—.

That voice… I glanced over my shoulder, only to find my beloved Rias glaring at Koneko and me with a forced smile and a dangerous aura.

"…P-Prez…"

"Fangzhongshu? Mating with different races? Negative influences?"
Sh-she heard everything?! Sh-she's going to murder meeeee!

As if that wasn't bad enough, Asia was right behind the prez! When had they shown up?!

The two of them should have been discussing things with the others in another part of the house until Koneko finished her treatment.

"...*Sniffle.* M-making a baby with Koneko now... I'm always getting left out..." Asia was very clearly holding back tears.

No, she's misunderstood completely! Did they only catch bits and pieces of our conversation and get the wrong idea?!

"Koneko, are you finished treating him?"

The prez's forced smile clearly terrified Koneko, who nodded silently. After managing a quick "G-good night," she fled the scene.

Nooooo! Don't leave me here like this! Konekooooo!

"Good. Now then, Issei. It's late, so how about we all go to bed? However, I'm afraid I can't let you sleep until you tell us what you were discussing with Koneko. Right, Asia?"

"Yes, Rias. You mustn't fall asleep until you've told us everything, Issei."

There was a strange weight behind their words as they dragged me into bed.

My interrogation continued until late into the night... Still, thanks to Koneko, my fatigue was completely washed away by sunrise.

–O●O–

The following morning, on my day off, I found myself waiting outside the convenience store by the station. Akeno and I had agreed to meet there.

Going on a date was certainly a nerve-racking experience. My heart was racing! I had taken special care with my appearance today. Even if Akeno and I saw each other practically every day, I still needed to dress properly.

I glanced around at my surroundings. The color of the roadside trees had started to turn with the coming of fall, but there were still lingering traces of summer weather. I was wearing long-sleeved casual clothes, but maybe I should have chosen short sleeves?

Just before our agreed meeting time of ten o'clock, a girl of a similar age to me appeared, wearing a cute frilly dress.

—!

"A-Akeno...?"

"Sorry. Were you waiting long?"

"N-no."

I blinked my eyes to make sure they weren't tricking me. My heart was thumping in my chest.

Akeno was wearing her hair down and was sporting typical clothes for a young woman her age. Plus, this was my first time seeing her in boots! Maybe I had been letting my thoughts get carried away, but I had expected her to wear something reserved and mature. This must have been how she dressed when out with the prez on casual business!

She truly looked like nothing more than a cute high school girl in those clothes! Based on her appearance alone, she could have been in the same grade as me—or even younger, for that matter.

Somehow, Akeno seemed even more beautiful than usual. I mean, she was always beautiful, but today she was especially so. Or maybe *cute* better described it?

That adorableness commanded all of my attention, and eventually, Akeno spoke up about it.

"Y-you're embarrassing me a little, staring at me like that... Is there something strange about the way I look?"

I shook my head vigorously. "You're super cute! Amazing!"

My straightforward opinion clearly left Akeno flustered with joy!

She would usually have given her characteristically mature *Oh dear* or *Oh-ho-ho*, but today, she seemed like an innocent maiden! It was a complete role reversal!

"Today, you're my boyfriend, Issei. So I'm going to treat you like one...for the whole day, okay?"

The way she was shyly glancing up at me with those upturned eyes was no fair! I couldn't resist this, and she knew it!

"P-please."

With my heart racing as fast as it was, that was as best as I could manage in response.

Even so, it was enough to make Akeno break out into a glowing smile. "Ah, I'm so glad. Thank you, Issei."

Her joyful expression was utterly adorable. This was bad. That simple look possessed deadly power!

Suddenly, I felt a murderous pressure cut short my sense of delight. When I cast my gaze over our quiet surroundings...

Wha—?!

...My eyes caught a flash of red.

Narrowing my eyes, I spotted a crimson-haired figure wearing large sunglasses and a wide-brimmed hat lurking behind a distant telephone pole. She was staring our way. Ah, and there was a tearful blond-haired girl wearing glasses. Behind her stood a petite figure with cat ears tucked under a wrestler's mask. Even farther back was a suspicious-looking guy with a paper bag over his head! Last of all was Kiba, dressed as usual, waving a hand apologetically.

Yep. It was the prez and the other club members. Had they decided to follow us in disguise?!

D-don't tell me they're planning to spy on our date?

"Oh dear. That's a bit of a crowd for an infidelity investigation, wouldn't you say?" Akeno, having noticed them, too, let out a soft chuckle.

As if to show off to the others, she drew closer to me. Her hair smelled so wonderful... I couldn't resist it...

Crack.

A dull sound echoed from behind me. Glancing over my shoulder, I realized that the prez, trembling with anger, had broken the telephone pole clean in half.

...Th-that was terrifying. It's probably best to pretend I didn't see that.

"Sh-shall we get going?"

"Please."

And so Akeno and I made our way into town.

We were now around three hours into our date.

All throughout, Akeno had acted like a typical girl her age. We went to clothing shops where she would ask, "Hey, Issei. Does this look good on me?" or "How about this one?" Even her usual catchphrases, *Oh dear* and *Oh-ho-ho*, were nowhere to be seen!

"It's delicious, don't you think, Issei?" Akeno inquired when we bought a crepe at a street stall.

We held hands as we walked through town. She was holding on so firmly that it was as if she was proclaiming her reliance on me! My heart wouldn't stop thrumming the whole time!

It was today when I realized how incredibly cute Akeno could be. Maybe she only showed this side of herself to someone she considered a boyfriend...?

Normally, this popular Japanese beauty maintained sophisticated mannerisms, a mature way of speaking, and an elegant and noble persona.

Yet right now, she was behaving like a complete teenager!

Anyone who saw her was sure to fall head over heels!

No, she was already bewitching enough in her usual form. And now, that cuteness was enough to KO a guy with a single glance!

If Akeno had a boyfriend, she would probably act this way while on dates with him. She didn't have such a lover at the moment, so she was using me as a substitute. One day, she would do this with someone else!

The moment I realized that, I found myself seething with jealousy at that future guy! Damn him! I was burning with envy!

That gave rise to a new idea in my mind—I wanted to have so much fun with Akeno today that any future boyfriend of hers would get jealous of *me*!

Thus, I took Akeno's hand in my own and declared, "Let's go to the aquarium today! And the arcade! We have to do everything!"

Akeno appeared shocked at first, but she quickly beamed. "Okay." She nodded.

Damn.

That smile of hers brought me low with just one shot.

Yep, you're seriously adorable today, Akeno!

"There are so many strange fish at the bottom of the sea," Akeno remarked happily as we left the aquarium.

We had visited the aquarium after having a bit of fun at the arcade. It hadn't been especially large, but it had a nice atmosphere about it.

Our hands were clasped the whole time, and whenever we saw an unusual fish, we laughed together.

To anyone watching us from afar…we must have looked like a pair of lovebirds. So lovey-dovey and absolutely smitten with each other! Ah, but it was so fun! This day was sure to go down as one of the best in my life.

Regrettably, a group of stalkers led by a certain crimson-haired figure had followed us around the whole time… I could feel the animosity radiating from them. I feared I wouldn't live much longer after this.

Akeno confirmed that they were still tailing us when we departed the aquarium. Then she flashed me a mischievous smile, pulled my hand, and took off at a dash!

Wha—?! What's happening?!

She glanced over her shoulder and joyfully declared, "Let's ditch Rias and the others!"

Although surprised, there was no way I could resist her, so I started running, too.

The prez must have known we would try to make a break for it, as she had hurried out from the building behind us!

Akeno pulled me right and left through the streets, hoping to shake off our pursuers.

After a few minutes, we turned onto an alleyway.

We emerged only after watching the prez and the others pass us by.

"Oh-ho-ho, I think we lost her." Akeno stuck her tongue out after our fellow club members. She looked as if she was truly enjoying herself.

Heh-heh-heh… I'm done for when all this is over. By the time the others were finished with me, I would probably wish I was dead…

Well, there was no helping that. So long as Akeno was having a good time, I was okay with whatever happened.

It was then I realized that Akeno and I had arrived in an unfamiliar part of town, likely because we hadn't really been thinking about where we were going. Just how far had we run?

I glanced around…only to find signs advertising rooms to rent by the hour for short rests…

Huuuuuh?! W-w-we're surrounded by…l-l-love hotels?!

How had we ended up *here* of all places?! Did the prez know we had come to this part of town?!

Uh-oh! I was in serious trouble now! If we didn't get out of here quickly, I was doomed!

"A-Akeno! W-we must have made a wrong turn somewhere. We should get going before—"

I tried to leave…only for Akeno to grab tightly on to my sleeve.

"…A-Akeno?"

Glancing over my shoulder, I saw that her face had turned bright red. She fidgeted nervously before murmuring, "…I'm okay with it."

…Huh? "Okay"…? Wh-what exactly does she mean…?

I didn't know how to respond to that, but Akeno looked determined and continued, "…If you want to go inside, I'm…I'm okay with it…"

…

My nose…blood was streaming out nonstop.

S-s-seriously?! Akenooooo?! Huh?! Really?! She's okay with that?! No fooling?!

She was all right with going to a love hotel with me?!

It would be to do more than rest, right?! She meant doing *that*, yeah?!

Akeno's usual erotic mannerisms were nowhere to be seen, completely replaced by the innocent fidgeting of a young maiden!

Whoa! Akeno! This new side of yours is so pure, so invigorating that I—I—I…! Can you do this, Issei Hyoudou?! This is Akeno we're talking about here! This might be your best chance! A-a short rest with Akeno before the prez finds us… My first time?! Whoooooaaaaa!

I had always thought my first time would be with the prez, yet was it destined to be with Akeno instead?! She had just issued me the most seductive of invitations!

I felt as if my masculinity was on the line here! Akeno looked to have made up her mind. Turning her down now would make me a failure as a man!

Could there be any greater happiness than spending my first time with Akeno?!

Was I up to it?! I needed to calm down! I would have to thank the Demon King for this incredible stroke of good fortune!

Just as I was about to make the most important decision of my life, a voice sounded from my side. "Geez, Red Dragon Kiddo. Trying to make love to a woman in broad daylight, are we?"

Huh? Who was that?

A casually dressed old man with a large hat had appeared out of nowhere, and behind him was a serious-looking woman wearing a pantsuit.

The woman was an incredible beauty. Her silvery hair was long and straight. You could tell how silky it was just by looking at it.

Leave me alone, old man. I have to decide whether or not to do it…

Huh? Something about the old geezer struck a chord in my memory.

"Heh, long time no see. It's me. I'm visiting from the North." The eye-patch-wearing geezer laughed with a lecherous grin.

I remembered that expression.

"Odin!"

Yep, he was the chief god of the Norse pantheon! I hadn't seen him since the incident with Diodora.

"Heh-heh-heh."

"Wh-what are you doing here?"

Seriously, why was he in a Japanese town? Sightseeing? Wasn't that a little reckless, what with all the recent terrorism?

Just as I was thinking as much, the lady with Odin cut in. "Lord Odin! W-we can't be seen walking around a p-p-place like this! Y-you're a god! You need to act like it!"

She looked so severe when she yelled at him. Ah, was this that armored girl whom I had seen accompanying him last time?

"Give me a break, Rossweisse. Part of your job is to entertain valiant heroes, no? So you had better learn the ins and outs of these kinds of places."

"You know I'm just an unattractive Valkyrie. And you two, what are you doing out here, and in the middle of the day, no less? Aren't you still in high school? Go home and study." For some reason, the Valkyrie—Rossweisse—redirected her frustration at Akeno and me.

Damn if that didn't ruin the mood. So much for deciding whether to go into the love hotel...

Fate sure could be cruel! I was crying on the inside!

At that moment, another man, who looked to be guiding Odin around, approached Akeno.

"...Y-you..." Akeno's eyes shot open in evident astonishment. Did she recognize this guy?

"Akeno, what are you doing here?" The man sounded furious. So much so that it bled into his voice.

"I-it doesn't concern you! Anyway, what are *you* doing here?!" Akeno countered, glaring back at the man.

Her innocent maiden persona from a moment ago had vanished in an instant. Just who was this man Akeno appeared to despise so thoroughly?

"What does that matter?! Get out of here! You aren't old enough for this kind of thing!" The man grabbed Akeno by the arm and tried to drag her away by force!

"No! Let go of me!" she cried out, fighting against him!

Hey, hey, hey! What the heck does this guy think he's doing?!

I quickly caught hold of the man, forcing him to release her. "I don't know what's going on here, but don't touch Akeno. Can't you see she doesn't like it? Besides, who are you to touch her?" I demanded, ready for a confrontation.

The answer, however, was something beyond expectation. "I'm escorting Odin around town today. The name's Baraqiel. I'm one of the leaders of the Grigori—and Akeno Himejima's father."

Life.2
Old Man Odin's Japanese Visit

"Oh-ho-ho. And that's why I'm here in Japan." The old geezer Odin laughed in the VIP room on the top floor of my family abode.

It sounded like he had business in Japan and so had decided to drop by our town. Given that this area was under the protection of demons, angels, and fallen angels alike, it was apparently a comparatively safe place to stay.

A god had come to visit my house…

Can you hear me up there in Heaven, Grandpa? This is amazing.

Every member of the Gremory Familia had gathered in the house. Azazel had joined us for the first time in a while as well.

In the end, my date with Akeno had come to a premature conclusion. We had ended up rejoining the prez and the others before leading Odin back to the Hyoudou residence. Akeno looked disappointed, but she seemed even more troubled by the encounter with her father. She was clearly in a bad mood. Her usual smile was nowhere to be seen.

Even though they were in the same room, she didn't so much as glance at her father, Baraqiel. Akeno's hatred for him must have run deep…

I had asked Azazel in passing once what kind of man Baraqiel was. Apparently, he was the stern warrior sort. Among the fallen angels, he stood shoulder to shoulder with Azazel in strength. It sounded like his attacks packed the biggest punch of any fallen angel, so they were undoubtedly powerful.

"Please have some tea," the prez said to Odin with a smile.

Heh-heh-heh. A short while ago, Rias had pinched my cheek as strongly as she could. I was in for a stern talking-to later. When I thought about it, I wanted to turn tail and run...

"Don't go out of your way for me. Ah, but they're as huge as I remember... So huge..."

That damn lecherous geezer... That filthy eye of his kept alternating between staring at the prez's breasts and Akeno's!

I would never forgive him if he dared to touch them! The prez's and Akeno's breasts were *mine!*

"Tch! Lord Odin, stop staring at them like that! She's the sister of the Demon King!" So saying, the Valkyrie hit the old fart over the head with a paper fan.

Odin rubbed the back of his head, his eye half-closed. Was it really okay for her to hit a Norse god like that, even if it was with a paper fan? That Valkyrie was incredible.

"You stiff-laced battle-ax. Sirzechs's sister is a renowned belle and comely to boot. Of course I want to look at her knockers. Ah, this is my Valkyrie attendant, by the way. Her name's—"

"Rossweisse. Thank you for your hospitality during our stay in Japan. It's a pleasure to meet you all."

After the geezer's introduction, the Valkyrie, Rossweisse, extended us all a formal greeting. She gave off a different impression now that she wasn't wearing her armor, but she was still undeniably beautiful. Was she around our age, perhaps?

She looked like a cool beauty, the kind who dependably set about to work despite her youth.

"She's a virgin. Been without a boyfriend for as many years as she is old." With a lewd expression, Odin gave us more information than any of us had asked for.

Rossweisse's face twisted in consternation. "Th-th-that's got nothing to do with anything! It's not like I *chose* never to have a boyfriend! Do you think I *want* to be a virgin? Y-you're awful! Aughhhhh!"

The stalwart Valkyrie collapsed to her knees. I felt a touch of sympathy for her. It looked like she and I had something in common.

I mean, it wasn't like I was girlfriendless by choice or anything...

Rossweisse had struck me as a cool and levelheaded beauty, but there was a huge gulf between her appearance and her personality...

"Well, the battle maiden industry is going through a bit of a rough spot. Even if they've got the looks, a lot of them haven't sprouted yet. The number of heroes has been dwindling lately, and so the Valkyrie department is getting downsized to cut costs. Basically, she wasn't in the best position when she started serving me, understand?" Odin explained.

Huh? I really didn't understand how things worked in the North.

Azazel let out a short laugh. "We'll watch your back while you're here in Japan. Think of Baraqiel as your backup from us fallen angels. I've been a little busy lately, and I'm out of town pretty often, so Baraqiel will keep an eye on things in my place."

"Indeed," Baraqiel added curtly.

Wait, is that why we're here, too? Are we going to be protecting Odin...?

"Still, aren't you a little early, old man? You weren't supposed to get here for a few days yet. You're here to see the Japanese gods, and Michael and Sirzechs are mediating, right? I asked to attend, too," Azazel remarked with a cup of tea in his hands.

"Well, that and the fact that I've been having little trouble at home... This upstart stripling keeps criticizing my way of doing things. I thought I'd move things along before he gets in my way. That's why I want to see the Japanese gods. We've had scant few dealings in the past." Odin let out a sigh as he stroked his long white beard.

So the Norse gods had problems of their own, did they? Well, I suppose it was natural for each faction to have one or two internal issues.

"By *trouble*, I'm guessing you mean the Vanir who's after your head? You'd better not go and bring Ragnarok down on us all...," Azazel said with a sardonic grin.

All those technical terms just flew straight past me.

"I don't care about the Vanir... Anyway, there's no point talking about it... By the way, Azazel my boy. I hear the Khaos Brigade is working on increasing their number of Balance Breaker fighters. Scary stuff. I thought that was supposed to be a rare phenomenon?"

—*!*

The members of the Gremory Familia exchanged startled looks. That was a rapid change of subject! Yet it sounded like we had been right. The Khaos Brigade *was* sending all those Sacred Gear users against us to try to unlock their Balance Breakers!

"Oh, they're rare, all right. Those idiots are trying to brute force an infrequent phenomenon in the crudest way imaginable. Anyone familiar with Sacred Gears would realize they *could* try doing it that way—but they wouldn't actually be stupid enough to attempt it. They'd be bombarded with criticism from every other faction. Whether it worked or not, they wouldn't escape that censure."

"'That way'? What do you mean?" I asked.

"Rias's report was basically on the money," Azazel began to explain. "Their strategy is to throw a whole lot of Sacred Gear users against the wall and wait to see which stick. First, they've been gathering humans with unique Sacred Gears from every corner of the world. Abducting and brainwashing them, for the most part. Next, they send them out to fight strong opponents. Then they repeat the process until a few Sacred Gear users reach Balance Breaker territory. Those who get that far are instantly teleported back to their home base. That shadow user you encountered the other day was one of those cases."

We were right. He did *reach his Balance Breaker...*

"There are certain things none of *our* factions were ever willing to do, even if we *have* considered them. Had I experimented with something similar back before we came to our peace accord, the angel and demon sides would have ganged up on the fallen angels for sure, and it would have been war all over again. None of us wanted that. However, these guys are terrorists, so they're willing to go to those extremes."

Basically, if anyone else were to treat Sacred Gear users like that, they would be attacked from every direction.

...*Hold on a minute. Wasn't my training to achieve my Balance Breaker somewhat inhumane, too...?* I had spent the majority of my summer vacation being chased around by a real-life dragon.

"You look like you're thinking your Balance Breaker training was similar," commented Azazel.

"That's because I am, Teach."

"Yeah, but you're a demon. You're tougher than the average human, you know?"

"I still almost died out there!"

"Ah, well, you're a tough one. We all knew that."

"Augh! Why do you always wave me off?! You're awful, Teach!"

Ugh, why was I the only one who had to put up with all this?! At this rate, I would become an antisocial delinquent!

"Anyway, abducting and brainwashing humans and then sending them into battle on the slim chance they may get stronger is a strategy employed only by the Khaos Brigade."

"What kind of people would do something like that?" I asked.

Azazel continued, explaining, "The core of the Hero Faction is made up of legendary warriors and descendants of famous historical champions. Their physical abilities are about on par with those of angels and demons. On top of that, they have their own Sacred Gears and other legendary weapons. They're capable of entering Balance Breaker modes and possess a god-slaying Longinus. According to our reports, the Hero Faction prefers not to use Ophis's serpents, so it isn't clear if they're doing anything to enhance their strength."

Power-ups or not, the Hero Faction's bosses sounded like formidable enemies. And was it really okay for warriors and heroes to resort to such inhumane training methods?

"The problem now is working out what they're hoping to do with their new Balance Breaker fighters," Odin said as he sipped his tea, his relaxed expression completely at odds with the gravity of the situation.

The old man must have been quite the optimist. Maybe I could even call him fearless? Just the other day, he had faced down a horde of middle- and high-class demons entirely by himself. But I guess that was to be expected of a god.

"Well, we're still looking into that, so there's no point speculating right now. More importantly… Anywhere you wanna go while you're in town, Gramps?"

Odin began to wriggle his fingers lecherously in response to Azazel's question. "The breast pub!"

"Ha-ha-ha, you know your stuff, Lord of the North! All right, let's get moving! I've had some young ladies from my own group set up an exclusive lounge here in town. How does a visit there sound?"

"Oh-ho-ho-ho-ho! That's the spirit, Azazel, my boy! You're a man of culture, I see! Get me girls with massive cleavage! I'll fondle them all!"

"Leave it to me, you decrepit old sleazebag! Welcome to Japan! You wanna wear a kimono with an obi sash? You've gotta try it at least once while you're here! I'll show you the real Japanese spirit!"

"I can't wait! Oh-ho, count me in!"

The two of them got themselves so worked up that they left the meeting early! What lecherous, perverted leaders they both were! Can you believe it?! That old fart was supposed to be the leader of the Norse gods!

To think that not only did the fallen angels choose the sex-obsessed Azazel as their governor, so, too, was that disgusting Odin the head of the Norse pantheon! The prez was holding her head in her hands, her brow twitching in apparent consternation!

I wanted to beg to tag along, but I stopped myself. That would only infuriate the prez even more.

"Lord Odin! I—I'll go with you!" Rossweisse cried out as she chased after them.

"You can stay here. I'll be fine. Azazel will be with me. Stay put, you hear?"

"I can't! I'm coming!"

Odin and his Valkyrie continued bickering all the way out into the hall. It looked like Rossweisse wouldn't take no for an answer.

Left behind in the room, we members of the Gremory Familia, along with Baraqiel, all let out resigned sighs.

"Akeno. We need to talk."

I had just been to the kitchen on the first floor and was making my way back upstairs when I heard a voice.

Up ahead, in the corridor on the fifth floor, I found Akeno and Baraqiel getting into some sort of argument.

"Don't you say my name like that." Akeno's voice was cold and sharp. It was a tone I had never heard from her before. She looked to be in a bad mood and wasn't wearing her usual smile.

"...What were you doing with the Red Dragon Emperor? Was that a clandestine meeting?"

This is about me?! Baraqiel seems furious! A-and a clandestine meeting? That sounds rather old-fashioned...

I knew it was rude to eavesdrop, but given that I was the topic of discussion, I was even more nervous about leaving.

"It's my life. What right do you have to meddle in it?"

"I've heard the rumors. He's a shameless dragon who takes nourishment from women's...b-breasts. People even call him the *Breast Dragon Emperor.*"

Had Baraqiel misunderstood about what we'd been doing?!

Taking nourishment from women's breasts?! That was crazy! What kind of weird rumors were people spreading?!

All I could do was hold my head in my hands at this shocking discovery.

"...*Ugh, give me a break, partner. How long do you want to keep torturing me...?*" Ddraig began.

Will you be quiet?! I'm not exactly enjoying this, either! I was willing to put up with being called Breast Dragon, but how will I be able to show my face in the underworld if people actually believe I feed off them?!

"*...Aughhhhh! Bwaaaaah!*"

Stop crying, Ddraig! You're going to get me going, too!

Breasts were supposed to be a side dish, not the main course!

"I'm worried that you let him treat you...indecently."

Ahhh, now I understood. This was simply a father who was worried about his daughter. Hold on. He didn't exactly look like such a bad person. What could have happened between him and Akeno...?

"Don't talk about him that way. Issei is...lecherous...but he's also kind and dependable. How can you judge someone based on nothing more than rumors? You're the worst. I knew it. I'll... I'll never forgive you..."

Akeno! She's vouching for me! I was so happy to hear her words that my eyes were growing wet.

"As your father—," Baraqiel began, but Akeno interrupted.

"Don't you start acting like a dad now! If you wanted to be my father, why didn't you come back for me?! How could you just stand by and let Mama die like that?!"

"..." Baraqiel fell silent at this barrage.

At that moment, Akeno spotted me in the shadows, our eyes meeting.

"Issei... Did you hear all that?"

She had found me out. It was my fault for eavesdropping, after all.

Feeling awkward, I stepped out from the dark.

Baraqiel's eyes lit up in rage. "Ngh! How shameless! For a man to eavesdrop on a woman! The rumors were true! All you care about is my daughter's chest! Isn't that right, you cursed *Breast Dragon Emperor*?!"

This misunderstanding was getting out of control!

I wanted to break down into tears! Akeno's father had the wrong impression of me!

Teach, this guy is your friend, right? Maybe you can help me out... No, that won't work!

Knowing Azazel, he would just find this whole misunderstanding hilarious and wouldn't lift a finger to help clear it up! Aughhhhh! I can see it now!

"What?! You're saying that the Red Dragon Emperor devours the breasts of young ladies, Azazel?!"

"Yeah, that's about it. He blows their clothes clean off 'em with a single touch, and then he whispers soft nothings to their breasts, getting 'em to talk back to him. You'd better watch out, Baraqiel. Akeno's could be next. Ha! Oh, don't take it so seriously, Baraqiel. Hey, can you hear me?"

"How absurd... He's a physical manifestation of the abstract, an enemy of womankind... A breast-devouring dragon... A-Akenooooo! Curse you, Red Dragon Emperor!"

I could picture the exchange between the two of them so vividly! Yep, that was more than possible! What was most scary was how well it all meshed with the rumors!

"I—I won't allow it!"

Cr-cr-crackle!

A wave of Holy Lightning coursed down Baraqiel's arm!

Whaaaaa—?! What's happening?!

Was he about to annihilate me all because of some mix-up?!

Suddenly, Akeno inserted herself between her father and me and embraced me.

"Don't touch him. Don't take him away from me. I need him... Just go away! You're not my father!" Akeno cried out.

Baraqiel's Holy Lightning dissipated at this outburst, and he closed his eyes. "...Sorry."

With that one word, he turned and took his leave. As I watched his well-built frame disappear down the hall, I thought he looked...a little sad.

"Akeno..."

She was gripping me tightly. She seemed to be holding back a torrent of indescribable emotions.

"Please. Don't say anything... Just let me hold you like this for a little while. Please, Issei..."

Her voice was trembling.

I had no idea what had happened between her and Baraqiel, but regardless...I gently embraced her.

-O●O-

The following day, the members of the Gremory Familia took part in a special event in the underworld sponsored by the House of Gremory.

"Yes, thank you."

It was a meet and greet, complete with autograph signings.

A long line of fans stretched out in front of us. I was busy scribbling my signature on one colored sheet of paper after another and shaking hands with the countless children who had come to see us.

The kids were overjoyed to receive my autograph, even though my writing in the demon script was terribly sloppy. They all broke out into joyous smiles when they shook my hand.

"Breast Dragon! You can do it!" they would call out to me.

Just watching it all made me feel like weeping in spite of myself.

Dammit, I was just so moved by all this!

If it was for the kids, I would be the Breast Dragon!

"The Switch Princess's breasts! Switch!"

"Kyargh!"

The prez was sitting beside me, signing autographs and shaking the hands of her fans, too, when a naughty kid poked at her bosom.

"Heeeeey! Don't you dare lay a finger on the prez's breasts! They belong to meeeee! Got that?!" I screamed in warning.

I wouldn't let him touch them! I wouldn't allow *anyone* to touch them! Those breasts were mine!

"Issei, he's just a child. There's no need to get jealous like that. I'll let you touch them later, so calm down," the prez said with a sigh.

Ugh, I mean, Prez... Your breasts are... Yes, please let me touch them later...

Evidently, the Switch Princess was popular as well.

Huh?

There was a long line of women stretching out in front of Kiba. Why couldn't that be me?!

Kiba's likeness was used for Darkness Knight Fang on the TV show.

He was one of the bad guy leaders, always dressed in a fancy suit of armor.

I wanted that kind of popularity! I'd forgotten after seeing how happy all the children were to meet me, but the real reason I put up with this nonsense was because I thought it would get me some hot moms. Yet Kiba had already stolen them!

Fine! But *I* was the Breast Dragon!

And Koneko, with her adorable beast look, was the Hellcat, one of my greatest friends and allies!

She apparently didn't mind that role, and she dealt with her fans politely.

What a professional!

After finishing the autograph session, we all made our way back to the dressing room tent.

The event was over, our mission complete!

Man, I was exhausted. I dispelled my armor, returning to my normal form.

No sooner had I done so than a staffer came up to me.

"Good work, Master Issei."

A young lady with her hair arranged in a roll down her back offered me a towel. It was none other than Ravel, Riser Phenex's younger sister.

"Oh, Ravel. Thanks." I took the towel, wiping the sweat from my forehead.

Apparently, when she had heard that we would be participating in this event, she had offered to help out.

"Th-this is part of my training! And I think that inspiring all of these children is a wonderful thing, so I wanted to help! I—I'm not doing it for you or the Gremory Familia, Issei!"

Odd protests aside, she appeared to be taking her job very seriously.

I couldn't say I fully understood Ravel's motives; however, I did know that she was a decent person. When I first met her, she had seemed to be on a bit of a high horse, but now, at least she spoke to me normally.

Every now and then, I thought she glanced my way with admiration in her eyes…but maybe that was my imagination.

"I'm starting to think it isn't so bad, giving these underworld kids something to dream about," I said.

"The children are crazy about you," Ravel replied.

"Yeah. They were all so excited to shake my hand. I feel like I've got to protect their dreams."

I didn't precisely know what I could do for them, but I wanted to be their hero, the Breast Dragon, for as long as I could.

"Issei, it's time we made our way back to the human realm," the prez called after peeking into my dressing room tent.

"Oh, right. We're supposed to be watching out for old man Odin today…"

That decrepit lecher had been ordering us around ever since he had shown up in town. He kept visiting that breast pub and even repeatedly tried to pick up women while out on the street!

I wanted to hit him over the head with a paper fan just like Rossweisse had!

"We should get going. You've had a long day, too, Ravel. Thanks again."

"N-not at all. I'm just learning." Ravel's cheeks turned pink in response to the prez's gratitude.

"Until next time, then," I said in parting.

"Yes. Do call whenever you're having another event. I—I'd be happy to help."

With that, the Gremory Familia made its way back home.

Ah, I couldn't wait until the next event!

With our underworld business completed, and having accompanied old man Odin around town for his Japanese sightseeing trip, Kiba, Gasper, and I were now training together in a mock battle.

I was in my Balance Breaker state, racing across the training field in a zigzag pattern using the propulsion unit on my back.

As a Knight, Kiba was much faster on his feet than I was. Nonetheless—

"Boost! Boost! Boost! Boost! Boost! Boost! Boost! Boost! Boost!"

If I multiplied my powers and pushed myself to my limits, I could race past him!

The propulsion unit was firing at its maximum output as I closed in on Kiba.

Claaaaaang!

With a swing of his Holy Demon Sword, he met my Ascalon head-on!

Clash! Cling! Claaaaaang!

We both hurried past each other swiftly, moving in every possible direction. Kiba never gave me an opening to attack.

...Dammit.

Fighting him with a sword had been a bad idea. Kiba was slowly pushing me back, his blade almost coming within range of my armor.

The speed of his Holy Demon Sword was increasing steadily! I couldn't fully follow its movements anymore. Once Kiba reached his top velocity, he would come straight for me.

Knowing that, my only option was to get in and use my fists!

Boom!

Once more, I ignited the propulsion unit on my back, hurling myself as close to that pretty boy as I could!

A short-range body blow! Unlike me, Kiba wasn't wearing any armor. In terms of defense, I had an unmistakable advantage. Not only that, but my attack power was superior, too. If I managed to strike him, my victory was all but guaranteed!

And yet—

Claaaaaaaang!

The sound of metal on metal rang out. Kiba swung his blade around horizontally, hitting me on the side of the head with all the force of a bowling ball.

He must have realized what I was trying to do and had launched a counter!

For a second, probably because of the jolt to my head, my consciousness faded and my vision got distorted.

Since Kiba couldn't get a direct blow on me, he had opted for a way to shock my body from outside my armor.

His counters were incredibly effective up close. I had fallen victim to them countless times over, as had Xenovia.

I was always on alert, but I could never predict from where or how those reversals would come. Kiba was always altering his strategy.

Still, I would never have imagined he would use the hilt of his blade like that... I had been convinced that moving near enough to punch would keep him from using his weapon properly, but it looked like I had been wrong...

I wouldn't be able to sustain another blow like that, so I moved to fall back as swiftly as possible.

Unfortunately, I quickly discovered that my feet were frozen to the ground and refused to budge.

"It's an ice-based Holy Demon Sword."

Sure enough, the blade in Kiba's hand was made of ice. He had used it to freeze me in place.

Bzzzzz!

A second Holy Demon Sword coursing with electricity appeared in Kiba's other hand.

A lightning one?! Is he planning on using that to shock me through my armor?! Sounds like it's time for my secret technique!

Whoosh!

A pair of red dragon wings shot out from my shoulders, each of them clawed like a pterodactyl's!

This was a new ability I could trigger after that whole Juggernaut Drive situation. I still couldn't use them to fly well, but I could manipulate them quite dexterously!

I moved my wings quickly and precisely, grabbing hold of Kiba's hands!

All right! Now he *can't move!*

"You've let down your guard!" I proclaimed.

Now that it was completely exposed, I drove my fist into his stomach!

Yet even though his arms were restrained, Kiba summoned another blade, this time from his right foot, and attacked with it! How long had he been able to make swords with his feet?!

Just as my blow was about to collide with that new blade, a heavy sound rang out.

"Th-that's it! Time's up! S-stoppppp!" Gasper was holding a large bell in his hands, jumping up and down in excitement.

Kiba and I halted our attacks before they connected.

Our practice matches all had time limits. Kiba and I both fell back, each of us wearing forced smiles.

Today's bout had ended in a draw.

"Your training is really too much for me sometimes, Issei," Kiba admitted with a laugh as he gulped down a sports drink.

After our mock battle, we had each set about our individual training regimens.

Kiba was taking a break. Meanwhile, Gasper was practicing on his own. He was trying to freeze a little robot Azazel had made that was darting around in the air.

I released my armor and squatted down beside Kiba, flashing him a wry grin. "I might have had insane power when I entered my Juggernaut Drive, but I can't use it anymore without dying. Still, if anything were to happen to Asia again... No, if any of you were in danger... But even if my Juggernaut Drive is off-limits, that doesn't mean I'm out of options. I'll just have to find another way to get stronger. Without inborn talent, all I can do is practice harder and harder. And since I don't have much demonic power, I have to draw on my stamina instead. I won't give up. That's how Sairaorg came to be the next heir in his family, right? If someone else can do it, why can't I?"

I had wasted most of my life span by using my Juggernaut Drive, but that didn't mean I would let what remained go to waste.

I couldn't afford to let the children see me like that, either. If the match between the prez and Sairaorg ever went ahead, it would undoubtedly be broadcast throughout the underworld.

I didn't want the kids to have to watch me put up a poor showing.

"Still, I can't beat you in terms of speed, Kiba," I replied.

Kiba shook his head. "When you boosted your rocket pack to dash toward me, you were just as swift as I was."

"Only because I was moving in a straight line. You could still probably dodge me most of the time. I would have to zigzag across the field like you to get past your defenses, but I can't reliably boost around like that. The best I can do is rocket forward."

"It's just a matter of getting the hang of it. Just so you know, that power of yours is much more than anything I can muster. And fighting the Red Dragon Emperor isn't easy. I get chills each time we face off. No matter how long I live, it won't be enough."

I appreciated the compliments. But all the same, defeating Kiba would be an arduous journey. With the way he mixed up his counters, I was never sure where to attack.

Lately, Kiba, Gasper, and I had been training together in a durable mock battlefield Azazel and Sirzechs had prepared. It was situated in a basement somewhere in the Gremory territory down in the underworld.

Given the potency of our abilities, Kiba and I had to refrain from going all out. If we were to seriously throw our all into these practice bouts, we could end up destroying the surrounding landscape or piercing it through with innumerable swords.

As such, it wasn't easy finding a suitable place for us to train.

Thus, Azazel and Sirzechs had given us this arena as a gift. Apparently, it was a reward for how well we had done against Diodora!

We'd had a special magic circle installed at my house to make the jump here directly. Some novel safeguards were placed on it so that the Khaos Brigade wouldn't discover the array.

It sounded like high-class demons who participated in the Rating Game had similar setups, but for us, servants of a young master who had yet to fight in any official matches, this was an unusual exception. Sairaorg was the only other exception.

The other members of the Gremory Familia used this training field often, too. This time, it was men only, so just the three of us had come.

"Do you think we're actually getting stronger...?" I asked Kiba while doing squats.

"Of course. It feels rude to say this, but you and I have already surpassed the president and Akeno. Either one of us could probably defeat an average high-class demon. But we can't afford to let our guard down."

"Yeah, a lot of people know about our abilities now, huh? They're probably all devising strategies against us..."

Kiba nodded.

Indeed, our performances during our last match had been widely broadcast throughout the underworld. Any potential opponents were undoubtedly studying our fighting styles to formulate counter-strategies.

My main weaknesses were that I couldn't respond to powerful attacks before completing my transformation and that anyone around me would be able to sense my strength building, since my aura increased proportionately with my strength.

As soon as someone realized I was powering up, they would recognize me as a threat and either try to avoid me or run away. What's more, if I went on to needlessly waste my energy, *I* would be out.

If I had to take off after a fleeing opponent, it might be okay to destroy the battlefield in a regular match, but if there were any special rules like when we had fought the Sitri Familia, that wouldn't be so easy.

Kiba's main weakness was his low defense, as nothing protected his body. His legs were his strength, but that also made them a kind of vulnerable spot, too. If someone were to aim for them, he would be done for. Yep, strategizing required deep consideration.

"For example," Kiba began between gulps of his sports drink. "There are Sacred Gears that can slow an opponent's feet, so if someone were to counter me with one of those, I would be in a dangerous spot. I hope I never bump into someone like that, but when it comes to actual battle, you never know."

An enemy like that was basically Kiba's natural predator, but I had a similar kind of problematic matchup.

"I'll have to be on alert, too, if we ever come across a dragon slayer."

"That's right. Even one hit would be dangerous. The Rating Game is all about compatibilities, so if we come across a dragon slayer, I'll handle them. I'll leave everyone else for you, though, of course."

I hadn't encountered a dragon slayer yet, but I wondered whether a blow from one of them would hurt as much as holy light did.

"C-c-c-can I help...?" Gasper inquired, timidly raising his hand.

"You're better off working with one of us rather than going it alone, don't you think?" I replied.

Kiba nodded. "Yeah. Gasper, your powers are best suited to a supporting role, so you can only really use them to their full potential when you pair up with another member of the Familia. Being demons, we have to acclimatize ourselves to team battles, and that means covering for each other's shortcomings."

"It's all well and good for one of us to get stronger, but there's no telling what a single person can do against a whole team," I added.

"Yes. You especially need to be cautious, Issei, seeing as you're hoping to branch out and become a King yourself one day."

"Heh. It's game over when the King is taken, right? Yeah, I'm not that stupid. I guess I'll just have to get used to group fights, then. But it wouldn't be too bad to be a King like Sairaorg..."

Kiba's eyes narrowed a bit at that in evident thought. "We'll have to develop a strategy to address him at some point, by the way. We could try to devise tactics to take him on one-on-one, but if we tried to engage him on his terms, we would be—"

"Eliminated, yeah. Ah, this demon life sure is tough! When I become a King, I'll have to remember to be careful."

Before we knew it, the three of us were deep in a conversation about battle plans.

Forcing through every issue blindly wouldn't get me anywhere. If I was going to have a future, then I needed to study like Kiba and the others. Thanks to them, I was starting to figure out how to talk about all these complex problems.

"Looks like you're wising up on tactics," said a new voice. I looked over my shoulder and found Azazel. "Here, dig in. The girls made you some rice balls."

We didn't waste a second before stuffing our faces with them. They were so delicious! Ah, I was sure Asia had made this one! It literally tasted of kindness.

Azazel sat beside us as we ate, letting out a chuckle. "I see you're toughening up there, Issei. Looks like all that training is working wonders."

"I still need to get stronger if I'm going to be the mightiest of Pawns, though. That's what I promised the prez. I need to keep my word before I can strike out on my own."

"By the way, I heard you're planning to take Asia and Xenovia with you when you go independent."

Did Asia tell him that? Or Xenovia, maybe? Truthfully, it didn't really matter where he'd heard it.

"Yeah, that's about right."

"Nice going."

"Well, I promised Asia we'd stick together forever. And I want to stay with her, too. Plus, doing my own demon stuff with Xenovia sounds fun, too..."

I never wanted to leave Asia.

Azazel patted me roughly on the head. "Sure, Issei. But if you're gonna be a King yourself one day, there's one thing you'd better remember."

"What?"

Azazel's face turned serious. "*Sacrifice.* You'll sometimes have to abandon your own pieces in a Rating Game. What will you do then? *That* will be what tests your worthiness to be a King."

"…Are you saying I should forget about helping them?" I pressed, but Azazel shook his head.

"Helping your comrades is fine. If you *can* save them, you should. But that isn't always possible in a real-life match. And seeing as defeated pieces get removed from the field, you'd have to be pretty unlucky to die during a Rating Game. That being the case, you might have to abandon a critically injured teammate for the good of the team."

"…That's a pretty harsh call," I muttered.

I couldn't abandon my friends. If they were ever in a pinch, I would rush to help them as fast as I could.

"There's no one in your Familia who cares more than you. That will be a liability in future Games—Kiba." Azazel's gaze abruptly turned my teammate.

"Yes."

"If you were in a match and had to choose between Rias and Issei, who would it be?"

"The president," Kiba answered without hesitation.

Yeah, that was the right decision. I would have hit him over the head if he had said otherwise.

I wasn't the most important member of our Familia when we were in a Rating Game. If we lost our King, it was over.

"Everyone else in your group had better realize the same thing," Azazel stated coolly. "Perhaps it's because your leader is a Gremory, but you're all unusually affectionate with one another. Frankly, you're right at the top in that regard when it comes to demons. You can use that as a weapon, but it's also a hindrance. If your rivals realize you're not willing to leave teammates behind, they'll build their strategy around that. And if you start losing because you keep trying to aid one another, your rank will suffer. You had better make sure you're ready to put the good of the team before a single teammate. Sona Sitri should have taught you the importance of that when you fought her group over the summer. I'm not telling you to abandon one another in real-life combat. However, if you're going to win Rating Games, you *will* have to do so there. You especially need to understand that if you intend to go independent, Issei. The only one who needs to survive till the end is the King—not your servants."

I need to be willing to give up my Familia members, huh?

There was no denying that Azazel was right. I had to make sure I understood that. And if this issue got me anxious when I wasn't even a King, how was the prez handling it all?

Prez. Would you abandon Kiba or me? Could you do that? If it means winning a Rating Game, I will gladly sacrifice myself.

Should the time come, I'd need to make my peace with that.

I was scared. The courage to throw away your comrades, to sacrifice them... I wanted to avoid that at all costs...

This required some thinking. I had to make sure I knew what to do when the time came.

Just what would I decide when I participated in my own matches as a King?

Ugh, first things first. I still needed to get promoted! Aughhhhh!

Maybe I was getting ahead of myself. I didn't even know when I'd be able to strike out on my own, after all! Vali had said that I would probably become a high-class demon within only a few years, but how could I be sure?

Argh! There was nothing to it but to keep improving, day after day! I would keep redoubling my efforts, moving forward one step at a time!

That said, our next match was fast approaching. I realized now what I had to do in our Familia's next Rating Game.

I took a deep breath before addressing my two companions. "Kiba,

Gasper. We had better make sure we're resolved to do whatever it takes."

Kiba nodded. "You mean to abandon our fallen comrades during the Rating Game, when necessary?"

"Yeah... We have to ensure the prez wins above all else."

Gasper, his lips still plastered with grains of rice, responded, "O-okay! W-we can do it!"

"Let's all make sure we're ready to go down with a smile for the prez! Still, we can't let ourselves be defeated until we've gone all out first! It would be uncool to try to shrink away from an enemy. So we'll stand up to them and fight, face-to-face, and only *then* will we be defeated."

My two companions nodded, both of them wearing broad grins.

"Yep."

"All right!"

If we were going to be knocked out of the fight, then we had to make sure we went out swinging—for the prez. We couldn't afford to abandon our desire to seize victory, either.

Azazel watched on beside us as he scratched his cheek. "That's cool and all, Issei, but you've got to do something about the way you fight women... Your Boob-Lingual and Dress Break techniques might be effective, but if you keep focusing on tricks like that, someone's going to work out how to get past you. Those abilities have some glaring shortcomings. What are you gonna do if you're up against a half-naked woman?"

"I'll rejoice!"

Azazel's shoulders slumped at my answer. "Nope. It's hopeless. You're done for."

It was true! If a sexy, half-naked lady appeared before me, I would totally lose control! Ah, and that's when they would come at me, once I had lowered my guard...

Hmm. I guess I'll just have to get used to all things erotic? No, that won't work!

There was no way I could just charge ahead while ignoring a sexy view!

I mean, if there were breasts in front of me, I would simply have to take a look!

Ugh. Well, whatever. Having finished eating the rice balls, I glanced across at Kiba and Gasper, both of whom were brimming with energy.

"All right, you two! Time for another sparring bout!" I declared.

Yep! This wasn't the time for thinking—it was time for training!

However, as I tried to encourage Kiba to fight me again, Azazel interjected, "Issei, come here."

He was wearing a lecherous expression. Clearly, he had come up with some new wild idea.

"What is it, Teach?"

"We've got another Breast Dragon test product. Take a look." Azazel retrieved something from his pocket.

"Wh-what is it…?"

In his hand was a small figurine.

"We're doing a Breast Dragon Emperor collaboration with a fast-food hamburger chain down in the underworld. You know, collectible toys bundled with the kids' meal. This one's of you. And this one's Rias, your Switch Princess."

The toy *did* resemble a deformed version of my Balance Breaker armor! And this crimson-haired figurine of the prez was a work of art! It was so cute!

"There's a special gimmick if you collect both of them. If you press the one of you to Rias's chest like this…"

"Oooooh."

—?!

The prez's voice rang out! What *was* this?! It was amazing!

"See? It makes a sound." Azazel puffed out his chest in pride.

"What is this?! I want one! Wow! This is going to be a hit!" I held the two treasures in my hands, my body trembling in awe.

They were amazing! These figures were sacred! I had no idea anything like this was even possible!

"Ha-ha-ha-ha! Even Sirzechs thought they were incredible! 'These toys will be epoch-defining!' That's what he said! I love coming up with ideas like this! Listen, Issei, if you want to become a high-class demon, you've gotta learn to value revolutionary concepts!" Azazel let out a dazzling laugh!

Incredible! I already knew he was a genius, but this surpassed all expectations...

It was a terrifying notion, indeed. Building a business on the premise of breasts... No wonder Sirzechs was so happy. The underworld's future looked bright!

Governor Azazel! The most charismatic of fallen angels! I was so glad we weren't enemies...

"Issei, breasts are the stuff of dreams. So how about we show them to the kids? Breasts are capable of fueling most any ambition."

"Y-yeah! There's no beating a breast-based business!"

I was repeatedly making the Rias doll squeal when Azazel's expression turned serious. "Can I entrust Akeno to you?" he questioned.

My eyes opened wide in surprise.

"You probably already know this, but Akeno hates Baraqiel, and the rest of us fallen angels, too," Azazel continued. "With Baraqiel here, I'm guessing she won't listen to me. If something happens, I want you to look out for her. I can count on you, right?"

"O-of course... But I still don't fully understand her situation," I answered.

"Do you *want* to know? Ah, but if I were to try to explain, it would sound like I'm trying to rationalize it all from the fallen angel perspective. I *am* the fallen angel leader, after all. Akeno's not liable to be impartial, either. You're better off asking Sirzechs or Grayfia. They'll be able to give you a more objective account."

Akeno was a member of the Gremory Familia. That being the case, it was likely best to ask someone familiar with the circumstances of each member of Rias's House.

"...You must have realized this by now, seeing as you're living under the same roof as her and all that, but Akeno is emotionally weak in some areas," Azazel said. "She maintains that elegant character most of the time, and the students at Kuou Academy adore her, but once you see past all that window dressing, what you've got is a teenage girl. You should have seen her when she watched you fall in battle against the Sitri Familia. The Queen is supposed to be the most composed piece on the board, but she started acting independently of her King in the middle of a fight."

I vaguely understood what Azazel was saying.

Akeno was usually so relaxed and sophisticated, with her *Oh dear* and *Oh-ho-ho* catchphrases. Every now and then, however, she would show an exceptionally maiden-like side, and at such times, she seemed incredibly fragile.

The Vestal of Thunder was a dependable young woman, but I couldn't help thinking that ultimately, she was no different from any other high school girl.

At least, that was how I felt. I had no way of knowing whether I was correct.

Azazel rested his hand on my shoulder, his eyes melancholy. "There will be times when she shows you that side of herself, so make sure you're ready to lend her a hand when she needs it."

"Wh-what do you mean…?"

"That will be what tests your worth as a man, Issei. Just so you know, a hug and a kiss can work wonders for making a woman feel at ease."

M-my worth as a man…

Wasn't that where I was most lacking?! If I was worth anything at all, wouldn't I be getting up to all kinds of erotic activities with Asia and the prez?! We slept next to one another every single night!

Was I completely spineless?! Was I incapable of reaching out when the most important spoils were lying directly in front of me…?! I didn't want to admit it, but could it be true?!

Whether I was or wasn't, becoming a harem king was still my goal! I could do it! I would show everyone!

Someday, I would be able to handle as many girls as I wanted!

"There's also the matter of your Juggernaut Drive," Azazel stated, suddenly changing the subject.

"I won't use it. I don't want to die."

"Yeah, that goes without saying. But you've awakened it now, so I'm thinking of looking into other ways to make use of the powers of the Red Dragon Emperor."

Was that actually possible?

"How?"

"Now that your Juggernaut Drive has been activated, it should have roused the thoughts and memories of the previous Boosted Gear vessels. I asked Ddraig to make sure, and it sounds like their negative emotions are trapped in your Sacred Gear. It's probably easiest to think of it like a curse. They're trying to reach out from the shadows to control you and make you go berserk so that the Sacred Gear can consume your life force."

"Th-that's…terrifying…"

Negative emotions…? A curse…? This Sacred Gear of mine was like something out of a horror movie…

Now that I thought about it, I still didn't understand a whole lot about how my Sacred Gear worked. I simply used its power when I needed to. It was still a big mystery.

"It's said that the friends and families of each successive generation of the Red Dragon Emperor have suffered misfortune because of that curse. I have a theory, however, that if we can purify those negative emotions, you might be able to bypass your Juggernaut Drive while still drawing on a similar level of power. By doing so, your life force would be safe. Pulling it off would mean diving deep into your Sacred Gear and finding a way to release all the dark emotions of your predecessors that have built up in there."

"S-so you're saying I need to soothe the lingering regrets housed in the Sacred Gear? And then a new power, something other than my Juggernaut Drive, will be born…?"

"Basically, yes. You'll have to put all the past Red Dragon Emperors to rest. Ddraig, help him out, would you?"

"That's all well and good, but the memories of past Red Dragon Emperors are so consumed by darkness that it's risky for me even to approach them."

"I'm guessing Issei Hyoudou, the Breast Dragon, will take care of that."

This was crazy! I still hadn't had so much as a chance to see whether I could even pull it off at all!

Not giving it a shot meant never using my Juggernaut Drive again, though. There seemed like little other option but to believe in Azazel's theory and try to find a new solution, then...

"Issei. I have faith in your potential. Every last Red Dragon Emperor was consumed by power and lost their lives because of it. You might be the most untalented Red Dragon Emperor in history, but you're the living embodiment of possibility. I mean, you unlocked your Balance Breaker by touching a woman's breasts and returned to your senses after going berserk thanks to them, too. You're a real-life Breast Dragon! And that's something. It's been a while since a dragon earned himself a new alias. Even if your physical strength and demonic powers are no match for Vali's or those of other legendary dragons, you can still take a different approach to using the Red Dragon Emperor's unique gifts to get stronger in your own way. All you need is effort, grit, and to forge an unlikely new path."

"Right!"

All I needed to do was put my faith in Azazel, Ddraig, and myself.

I would get stronger and find my own way.

And instead of being used by this Sacred Gear, I would use *it*!

The man who most understood the Boosted Gear.

Yep, that kind of title would be awesome.

I resumed my training with Kiba and Gasper, more pumped up than ever.

Several days had passed since Odin first joined us in Japan.

The members of the Gremory Familia, Azazel, the old man, and

Rossweisse were riding in a carriage pulled by Odin's eight-legged warhorse, Sleipnir.

It was flying straight through the night sky!

What's more, the carriage was huge, probably because the warhorse itself was so large.

Kiba, Xenovia, Irina, and Baraqiel were soaring outside as escorts. After all, we could be attacked be terrorists or who knew what else at literally any moment.

"Ah, I love a good *Yamato nadeshiko*... And there's no beating geisha girls..." That old geezer Odin was chortling to himself under his breath, his expression one of total satisfaction.

Damn him!

And he was using us as a band of bodyguards! He'd been dragging us all around Japan with this giant warhorse of his. We had been to hostess clubs in Tokyo, an amusement park, and even sushi restaurants. We were seeing Japan through the eye of that old clod.

Because we high school students were still minors, there were a lot of places we couldn't enter, leaving us stuck in the waiting room until he returned.

That old fart! Damn him!

Had he at least let me enter one of the hostess clubs with him, I wouldn't have hated him so much!

Glancing around, I saw that the other club members all looked exhausted. Asia was resting her head against my shoulder, sound asleep!

Akeno...seemed preoccupied. Her aura was practically a warning light telling me not to try to speak to her.

Taking care of Odin sure was a pain in the ass. Whenever he got mad, he would say something like "I can't hear you," or "Azazel, are my breasts ready yet?" He was unbearable!

And yet he was an important guest, so we had to accompany him everywhere without complaint.

"Lord Odin! It's almost time for your meeting with the Japanese gods, so please, let's forget about sightseeing for now. At this rate, we'll both be yelled at when we get home!" Rossweisse had calmly suffered the old man's indulgences for the past couple of days, but she looked to be at the end of her patience, ready to slam her head against the wall.

"Geez, you don't know how to have fun, do you, woman? Relax a little. No wonder you haven't been able to find yourself a man."

"Th-th-this has nothing to do with whether or not I have a boy-friend! I—I'm not single by choice! Aughhhhhh!"

Ah. She's broken down into tears again. These Norse folk truly were annoying... Maybe I could come up with some excuse to go home early...?

Cr-crash!

Neeeeeigh!

With no warning, the warhorse came to an abrupt halt. The carriage lurched forward, taking us with it.

We were all caught unprepared.

"What's going on?! A terrorist attack?!" Rossweisse cried out.

"How should I know?! This kind of thing is never good!" Azazel responded. His voice sounded tense.

That noise a moment ago must have been the horse. Something must have happened to the huge creature.

I glanced outside the window and found Kiba, Xenovia, and Irina positioned around Baraqiel, ready for battle.

I...still couldn't fly. Sure, I could make my demon wings appear, but I couldn't use them to soar through the air.

Even Azazel had made fun of me for that. *"It's kind of funny how you unlocked your Balance Breaker before even learning to fly,"* he had teased. Admittedly, I *had* done things in a pretty unusual order.

The best option was to open my wings while I was in my Balance Breaker state. Then I could leave the actual flying to Ddraig.

I really needed more training—in flying most of all. No matter how far I boosted my powers, if I couldn't do that much, I would just end up letting down all those kids in the underworld.

I opened the window and looked outside with Prez and the others.

At the same time, I began my Balance Breaker countdown. There was no telling what might happen, so it was best to plan for the worst.

There was a young man floating in front of us. He was a complete pretty boy, with a vaguely sinister cast to his features.

He was wearing a robe similar to the one Odin donned for formal occasions. This one, however, was black in color.

Having presumably recognized who this guy was, Rossweisse wore a stunned expression. Azazel even clicked his tongue.

Wh-who is this guy...?

The man lifted his cloak, sneered, and called out, "Greetings, everyone! I am Loki, the malicious god of the North!"

...M-malicious god? If he's from the North, does that mean he came from the same place as Odin?

Everyone but me was on edge, as though watching in disbelief. Azazel unfurled his black wings and stepped out from the carriage.

"...Loki. One of the Norse gods," the prez whispered by my side.

—.

So he is a god?! Seriously?! I-in that case, he really is from the same realm as Odin...

What was he doing here? Something told me that whatever it was, it couldn't be good.

"If it isn't Lord Loki. Strange seeing you here. Do we have business? The chief god of your Norse pantheon is riding with us in this carriage here. However, I'm guessing you must already know that," Azazel stated calmly.

Loki crossed his arms as he responded. "It's painful to watch. Our esteemed leader, the head of our great mythological system, is turning his back on us to have dealings with beings from other faiths. I came here to put a stop to it."

What a declaration! He sounded totally like a villain!

At this, Azazel's tone of voice changed to one filled with anger. "You don't beat around the bush, Loki."

I knew how much Teach enjoyed his peaceful everyday life. He must have seriously resented anyone who threatened it.

Evidently amused, Loki laughed. "Bwa-ha-ha-ha, if it isn't the governor of the fallen angels. I wouldn't normally deign to meet with you or those demon companions of yours. Regrettably, I had no choice this time. All of you will be purged along with Odin."

"It's okay for *you* to interact with beings from other systems, but not Odin? Seems a little contradictory from where I'm standing."

"There's nothing wrong with *destroying* beings from opposing organizations. I don't accept your proposal for peace. It was *your* system that invaded *our* soil, spreading the word of your repugnant Holy Bible."

"...There's no point complaining to *me* about that. Bring it up with Michael or the late Christian God," Azazel replied, scratching his head.

"In any event, Odin's fraternizing with the gods of Japan cannot stand. At this rate, Ragnarok, which we should all be eagerly awaiting, may never come to fruition. What do you hope to gain by trading information on Yggdrasil?"

Azazel pointed to Loki. "Let me ask *you* something! Are you working with the Khaos Brigade? Ah, but I guess I shouldn't expect a trickster god like you to answer truthfully, huh?"

Loki seemed unamused by the inquiry. "I'm disgusted that you would conflate me with those witless terrorists. I came here of my own volition. Ophis has nothing to do with this."

Only now did Azazel relax. "...So you aren't with them. I guess this is a separate issue, then. Okay, old man. This must be that *thing* you were going on about."

Just as Azazel glanced back toward the carriage, Odin and Rossweisse stepped outside.

Odin activated a magic circle beneath his feet, using it to float through the air. "Hmm. Yes, we still have a few stubborn holdouts—fools like this clown," he said while raking his fingers through his beard.

With a flash, Rossweisse's business suit changed back into a set of armor. "Lord Loki! You're overstepping your bounds! Showing aggression to your chief god is unforgivable! If you have a disagreement, you should raise it during an official council session!"

Loki, however, didn't show any intention of hearing out Rossweisse. "Mere Valkyries should remain silent, for I am speaking to Odin. Are you set on continuing this course of action, which exceeds the bounds of Norse mythology?"

Faced with a clear threat, old man Odin answered coolly, "That's right. Sirzechs and Azazel are a thousand times more interesting conversationalists than you. I'm curious about Japanese Shintoism. And *they're* interested in our Yggdrasil. Once we officialize relations, I'm thinking of starting some cultural exchanges."

Loki's lips contorted into a bitter smile. "...I see. How foolish of you. Perhaps we should welcome the Twilight of the Gods here and now, then?"

A chill ran down my spine, and my skin began to tingle in the face of an overwhelming sense of hostility!

Loki stared across at us—no, at Odin!—with raw spitefulness!

"Shall I take that as a declaration of war?" Azazel questioned.

Loki scoffed. "Take it how you will."

Boooooooooom!

Out of nowhere, a powerful wave of energy slammed into him.

I glanced around and realized that Xenovia had struck with Durendal. The Holy Sword was emanating a powerful aura.

"Victory goes to the one who makes the first move. Isn't that what they say?"

She said that so calmly! Wow, Xenovia! Talk about a flying start!

"I guess it wasn't particularly effective, though," she added quietly after a moment. "I should have expected as much from a Norse god."

Indeed, Loki continued to float there as if nothing at all had occurred.

Seriously?! Xenovia's attack didn't hurt him one little bit?!

"A Holy Sword? I'll grant you that it has impressive power, but you'll need quite a bit more to take on a god. You might as well have struck me with a gentle breeze."

Kiba called forth one of his Holy Demon Swords while Irina similarly formed a blade of holy light.

Loki regarded this only with clear amusement. "Bwa-ha-ha! How futile! I'm a *god*! Attacks from angels and demons are nothing to me." With that, he slowly raised his hand toward us.

I could sense it instinctively. There was some unknown force building in his palm.

We would be in trouble if he unleashed that energy!

"Welsh Dragon: Balance Breaker!"

My countdown had finished! A red aura wrapped around me, solidifying into a suit of armor!

Ddraig! I'll leave the flying to you!

"All right, partner."

I leaped from the carriage just as my Balance Breaker activated, accelerating toward Loki at incredible speed!

"Jet!"

A sound echoed from the jewels studding my armor, just as the propulsion unit on my back ignited!

Swoosh!

I raced toward Loki, but he easily avoided my oncoming punch. My fist flew clean past his nose!

"Prez!" I cried out. "I need a Promotion!"

With Rias's consent, I Promoted to a Queen! I could feel the added strength flowing through me!

"I see. I almost forgot. The Red Dragon Emperor is among your members. Your strength is to be commended. However..."

Particles of brilliant light gathered in Loki's hands! I could see them with my naked eyes! He was compressing an overwhelming mass of power, preparing to launch it straight at me! A direct hit from that would be bad!

"…You aren't quite ready to take on a god!"

I hurled the most powerful Dragon Shot I could muster into the energy speeding out from Loki's hands!

"Boost! Boost! Boost! Boost! Boost! Boost! Boost! Boost! Boost! Boost!"

Boooooooooom!

The two energies collided in midair, ricocheting violently off each other! The impact caused an explosive burst of wind, buffeting me and the others! I had put my all into that attack, yet Loki had broken through as though it were nothing! This must have been the might of a god!

Red smoke rose up from Loki's hand. It looked like my Dragon Shot had managed to do something, at the very least.

Loki glanced down at his hand, his lips curling in a grin. "…I wasn't exactly holding back just then. Interesting. You don't know how happy I am to see this. It's certainly worthy of a good laugh! Bwa-ha-ha-ha!"

I wasn't happy at all! Loki was definitely going to be a formidable opponent!

From the looks of it, even the powers of the Red Dragon Emperor would have a hard time matching a full-blown deity!

The prez and Akeno unfurled their demon wings before jumping out of the carriage. The prez was engulfed in her crimson aura, ready for battle.

"Crimson hair. The House of Gremory, I presume…? The blood of the present Demon King, yes? A coterie of two fallen angel leaders, one regular angel, a horde of demons, and the Red Dragon Emperor. For an armed escort, you've gone a little overboard, Odin."

"And yet you still came, fool that you are. All this protection was the right call."

Loki nodded at Odin, the smirk on his face widening. "Very well. Then I, too, shall call for support." With that, he spread his cloak and bellowed up into the sky: "Show yourself! My dear son!"

There was a short pause—followed by a rift opening up in the air.

What's going on? Who did he summon?

"Owoooo!"

Appearing from the spatial tear was an ashen-colored dog! No, a wolf!

It was gigantic, at least ten meters from head to tail, and it positioned itself directly in front of us!

Wha—? Wh-what is this...? My whole body was filled with terror just by looking at the wolf!

The moment its gaze fell on me, I was unable to move a muscle, completely paralyzed.

A cold shock coursed through my flesh. Fear, murderous intent, and horror gripped my heart.

It was freaky! My hands were actually shaking!

Forcing myself to look around, I realized that the other members of Rias's Familia were equally affected. Even the most dauntless of us were terrified by this overwhelming wolf!

Wh-what on earth is it...?!

The wolf showed no sign of moving. It simply continued to glower at us with its piercing eyes.

"...That creature is dangerous, partner. If you can, you should avoid fighting it."

Even Ddraig, the fabled Red Dragon Emperor, was wary.

That *thing* was no run-of-the-mill enemy... It even looked more intimidating than Loki himself!

"This is bad... Everyone, keep clear of that huge wolf! Issei, fall back!"

Azazel looked more uneasy than I had ever seen before. Our bold and daring teacher, who hadn't so much as flinched when facing the old Demon Kings, was now visibly scared...

"Teach! What *is* that wolf?" I asked.

"Fenrir," Azazel responded, his voice sounding as though it had been squeezed out of him. "The God Eater."

"—?!"

Every last one of us was startled at this revelation. Yet there was no doubting it was true.

"Fenrir! Impossible! Not here!"

"…This *is* bad…"

Kiba and the prez seemed on edge. Evidently, they had heard of this wolf before.

Clearly, the beast was dangerous, but there had to be more to it than that!

"Issei! That is one of the most evil and dangerous monsters in existence! His fangs are capable of killing a god! Not even your armor will be able to protect you!"

Seriously?! This wolf is really that dangerous?! Capable of slaying a god?! How is that at all fair?! No wonder Ddraig told me to steer clear of him!

I had a hunch that even if we attacked together, it wouldn't be enough.

"That's right," Loki said calmly as he patted Fenrir's back. "You should be cautious. This is one of the greatest creatures I've ever developed. His fangs can strike down a god. I've never had a chance to test it, but they should be equally potent against gods or similar beings from any of the other religious systems. And they're just as fatal to high-class demons and legendary dragons, too."

Gulp.

Loki leveled an accusatory finger at the prez. "To be honest, I don't much care for the idea of siccing Fenrir on anyone outside the Norse pantheon. But having him taste the blood of outsiders might be a good learning experience for him."

That bastard. He can't seriously be planning to—

Loki interrupted my thought to confirm my morbid suspicion. "A lick of Demon King blood will surely be of use to Fenrir. Go."

"*Owoooooooooooo!*"

In the dark of night, that ashen wolf let out a terrifying howl.

That noise was enough to make our bodies tremble. Its sound was so resonant that our hearts were caught in rapt attention.

Swoosh.

There came a burst of wind. The wolf, which had been right in front of me, was gone.

At that moment, my body moved faster than my thoughts!

"*Jet!*"

Not on my watch! I wouldn't let him!

Not the prez! Not my beloved—

"Don't you touch herrrrrrrrr!"

Whoosh!

I dashed to place myself in front of the prez before the wolf could reach her and thrust my fist right into the beast's face!

…

Even I was left shocked by what I'd done!

My body had basically moved by itself!

All I knew was that the wolf had been going for the prez. My only thoughts had been to protect her! And before I knew it, I had dealt the creature one hell of a punch!

"Issei…" Rias looked just as astonished as I was.

"P-Prez! Are you okay? You aren't hurt?"

"N-no, I'm all right. Thanks to you."

I breathed a sigh of relief.

I wasn't entirely sure how, but it looked like I had been able to protect her. There was no way I would let that damn wolf gnaw my Prez to death!

As for Fenrir himself, he had been staring at me coolly since I'd hit him, but he took no other action.

Was my punch ineffective? Damn, what a sturdy monster.

"Gah!"

Blood spurted from my lips.

Wh-what…?

Only then did I notice something was wrong with my body. I glanced down and saw a gaping hole in the armor around my abdomen.

Upon realizing what had happened, I vomited up more blood. Excruciating pain coursed through me.

"Issei!" the prez and Akeno shrieked in unison.

My stomach felt hot… Trust me when I say it hurrrrrrrrrt. When had I taken a hit…?

Glancing back at the wolf, I realized that his left forepaw was drenched in crimson.

Had he clawed through my armor at the same moment I had hit him in the face…?

My entire body staggered in midair.

Just before I could collapse, Kiba caught me. "Issei. Hang in there. Asia, heal him, now!"

"Issei! Hurry!" Our healer, Asia, cried out to me from the carriage. She was generating a healing aura in her hands. She must have been trying to heal me from a distance.

"I don't think so. Even if only for a second, you matched Fenrir's movements, Red Dragon Emperor. Truly frightening. It's best you're dealt with now." Loki motioned to give Fenrir further instructions.

This was bad!

I wouldn't be able to escape! If I did, the prez would end up taking the blow! I couldn't allow that! I had to protect her!

I didn't want to die! I was terrified! More than anything, though, I wouldn't be able to live with myself if Rias Gremory perished instead!

"Lokiiiii!"

Azazel hurled a spear of light at the god while Baraqiel unleashed a barrage of Holy Lightning.

"Even without Fenrir, two fallen angels can't hope to defeat me."

A magic circle of a design I had never seen before formed in the sky, shielding Loki. Azazel's and Baraqiel's strikes were easily blocked.

"—! Norse magic! Right, their spells are more advanced than those used in the Christian religion! Their entire system is rich in sorcery!" Azazel spat in disgust.

The two fallen angel bigwigs had attacked simultaneously, but even that hadn't worked!

Could a god really be this powerful?!

"In that case, I'll use the same techniques!"

Shing!

Rossweisse deployed several magic circles similar to that which Loki had just used, releasing a seemingly inexhaustible magic attack! It was a full-on barrage!

What incredible destructive output! Rossweisse was clearly quite the fighter! Then again, she *was* Odin's bodyguard, so it wasn't all that surprising that she was so exceptional in combat.

Amazing. I had no idea she was so skilled in magic, I thought.

Brrrrr-rrrrr-rrrrr-rrrrr-rrrrr!

Loki's defensive magic circle deployed to shield his whole body, protecting him from each of Rossweisse's attacks!

Not even the same kind of magic can get through to him?!

"My turn." Loki swung his arm to one side.

Fenrir's murderous aura increased in turn. The wolf's cold, emotionless eyes fixed themselves squarely on us.

Koneko and Xenovia stepped in to shield me and the prez. I wanted to tell them to stop, that it was pointless. That wolf had pierced clean through my armor! They wouldn't be able to stand against him!

My friends were about to get themselves killed!

I couldn't stand it! At this rate, we would all be annihilated! We couldn't meet our end like this!

Just as it all seemed hopeless, a brilliant flash overtook all else.

It pierced through the wolf practically at the speed of light.

"*Half Dimension!*"

"*Gwaughhhhh!*"

The space around Fenrir began to distort. The creature had been boxed in and rendered unable to reach us.

Nonetheless, he quickly began to fight against his trap with fangs and claws.

A silver light streaked down from above, settling between the wolf and us.

"Issei Hyoudou, are you all right?"

"Vali…"

Yep, in front of us was none other than the White Dragon Emperor, Vali!

I thought I had recognized that attack, and sure enough, it had been him!

Vali's technique was capable of halving any target within range. Yet Fenrir was so powerful that all it seemed to accomplish was restraining the creature for a few moments!

"Hey, hey! Is the Breast Dragon dying? Damn, I can't even tell if he's super strong or super weak anymore!"

Accompanying Vali was a figure riding atop a golden cloud—Bikou. *What are these two doing here?* I wondered.

"Ah, the White Dragon Emperor!" Loki seemed truly excited by Vali's entrance.

"Greetings, Loki, God of Evil. I'm Vali, the White Dragon Emperor. And I'm here to slaughter you."

The declaration didn't look to ruffle Loki in the slightest. Rather, he seemed pleased.

"The Two Heavenly Dragons are more than enough for me. I think I'll fall back for now!" So declaring, Loki recalled Fenrir. With a twirl of his cloak, the air distorted around the Norse god, enveloping him and his creature. "But hear this! I will return on the day of your meeting with the gods of this land! And I shall put a stop to your plans, Odin!"

Just as Loki and his wolf made their exit, my consciousness, too, began to leave me.

I had lost a lot of blood.

Asia was bent over me when I came to, using her Sacred Gear to heal my injury.

Her warm green aura flowed through me, taking away the agony that had been racking my body.

"…Thanks, Asia," I managed weakly, looking her in the eyes.

Seeing that I had woken up, Asia shed a tear. "Issei! Thank goodness!" She wasted no time embracing me.

"You didn't really expect me to die and leave you all alone, did you?" I replied, hugging her back.

"...I'm glad you're all right, Issei," came Koneko's soft voice.

Had she stuck by my side, too? Her hands were wreathed in *qi*, so she must have been using her sage magic abilities to strengthen my body's recovery.

"Thank you, Koneko," I said, patting her on the head.

"...*Meow*. Issei..."

"Yep. I'm okay now... Where are the prez and the others?"

It was just the three of us inside the carriage.

Koneko answered, "Rias is talking to everyone outside... Including the White Dragon Emperor."

Right. Vali showed up toward the end of our encounter with Loki.

I carefully stood and peeked out from the carriage. It had already landed in a park near Kuou Academy. As it was still the middle of the night, no one else was around.

While making my way to the prez, Azazel, Odin, and the others, I heard Vali talking.

"I'm guessing you're going to need to defeat Loki if there's any chance of Odin's talks being a success." He cast his gaze over everyone. "Your assembled ranks and the Red Dragon Emperor won't be enough to surpass Loki and Fenrir. And given the Hero Faction's constant incursions, the underworld, Heaven, and Valhalla all have their hands full. They won't be able to devote any more resources to help."

None of us could argue that point.

Vali then turned his gaze to me and flashed a grin. Noticing that, everyone else looked in my direction, too.

"Issei! How are you feeling?"

"I'm all right now, Prez. More importantly, though..." I narrowed my eyes at Vali.

Only now did I realize that Bikou and his companion with the Holy

King Sword—Arthur, I think his name was—were standing behind him. It looked like the three of them were waiting to see how I would act.

"Are you saying *you* can beat him?" I questioned in a low voice.

Vali shrugged. "Unfortunately, in my current state, not even I'm strong enough to fight both Loki and Fenrir together."

All that tough-guy talk a second ago, and *he* was no match for Loki, either?

"However…," Vali continued, still staring right at me. "It would be a different story if the Two Heavenly Dragons fought together."

"—!"

Everyone, myself included, gasped at the suggestion! We weren't the only ones, either. Vali's two companions were equally stunned!

Was there any other way to react? I don't think anyone could have anticipated that Vali would propose that! We were so taken aback that no one responded.

"I'm saying I'll fight beside you this once, Issei Hyoudou."

Life.3
A United Front!

The following day, we all gathered together in the spacious hall in the basement of the Hyoudou residence.

We members of the Gremory Familia were joined by Irina, Azazel, Baraqiel, the Sitri Familia...and Team Vali. There was a heavy awkwardness about the room as we all took seats around a table.

It felt weird to host Vali and Bikou in my own home. The prez had been adamant against them coming here, but after hearing out Azazel and Sirzechs, she had reluctantly acquiesced.

Sirzechs, why did you let these guys step foot in my house?

Did it have something to do with them helping rescue Asia? That couldn't be it.

Why would Vali and his goons want to team up anyway? What did they get out of it?

Vali had claimed it was for defeating Loki, but had he been honest? I had no way of confirming.

Old man Odin and Rossweisse were in another room, contacting their homeland.

Loki's presence in Japan must have been causing a big stink for the Norse gods, too.

In any event, our discussions about how to handle Loki were already underway.

The Demon King Sirzechs was already aware of the situation. All vital information had also been conveyed to Heaven and other underworld officials, too.

The three great powers had agreed to work together to ensure the success of old man Odin's meeting with the Japanese gods.

That said, they had essentially agreed that those in this room were already used to working together, and so *we* would be the ones actually to handle the issue.

In other words, the higher-ups had ordered us to take on Loki alone.

Our opponent was a deity, yet the more significant issue was that giant wolf of his—Fenrir.

That monster's powers had surpassed even those of his creator. From what I heard, Fenrir's abilities were comparable to the Two Heavenly Dragons before they had been sealed away in their respective Sacred Gears. Not even Azazel or Tannin would be able to defeat him alone.

Of course, Vali and I still couldn't fully draw on the original strength of the Two Heavenly Dragons. The fight was over before it began.

There was a possibility of success if we used our Juggernaut Drives, but if I did that, I would die. Vali would end up exhausting his demonic powers, and even if he did manage to defeat Fenrir, he wouldn't last long against Loki in that state.

We might have a chance if everyone else was willing to put their lives on the line, but there would inevitably be sacrifices.

Casualties were expected going in.

Unfortunately, there was little hope of reinforcements. The Hero Faction was still sending out its Sacred Gear and causing disarray, sowing chaos among all factions.

The three great powers and the Norse gods were on maximum alert and were unable to divide their forces.

Knowing that, our priority was to find an alternate approach that would involve as few sacrifices as possible.

"You first, Vali. What's your reason for helping us?" Azazel, standing in front of a whiteboard, asked the question that was on everyone's minds.

Yep, we all wanted to know why he was aiding us. It felt so weird.

Vali's lips curled in a fearless grin. "I simply desire to fight Loki and Fenrir. Bikou and the others have already agreed to help. Is that not enough?"

He truly was battle-obsessed! How crazy did you have to be to *want* to throw yourself into harm's way?!

Azazel frowned at the response. "Yeah, that isn't enough. I can't deny we need your help, however. Thanks to the Hero Faction, we've got no reserves to spare. Some are concerned that your actions might be connected to those of the Hero Faction… But knowing you, I doubt you'd cooperate with people like that."

Had Vali's suggestion been meant as a threat? Team up and defeat Loki together—or don't team up, and he would fight us all one by one to build up enough experience to defeat Loki afterward?

"Sirzechs also considered our options, but in the end, he decided he couldn't dismiss an offer of assistance from a descendent of a former Demon King. He's definitely got a naive streak, but I agree that it's better to have you working with us than roaming free."

"This is only temporary. There's still much about you we can't condone," the prez interjected.

It looked like she had a fair number of complaints lined up, but since her older brother had already rendered his judgment, she was unable to voice them.

Chairwoman Sona, too, looked to be of a similar disposition. Judging by her expression, she was also dissatisfied.

Keeping an eye on Vali and his allies was better than letting them act as they pleased, but it probably wasn't best to say that to their faces…

Begrudgingly or not, the prez had agreed to this, meaning I would have to do so, too. However, if Vali did anything weird, I wouldn't stop myself from hitting him.

Asia, ever the saint, didn't look like she had too many qualms about accepting help from terrorists. Vali *had* saved her life. The rest of the Gremory Familia regarded the situation about as well as Rias, but they must have accepted things for the moment, as they all remained quiet.

Azazel continued to stare intently at Vali. "You're up to something, aren't you?" he pressed.

"Who knows?"

"Any suspicious movements, and I think we'd all be warranted to cut you down."

"I have no intention of doing anything fishy. But anyone who attacks me will come away from it with far more than a warning," Vali replied, his grin unwavering.

"…Well, let's put that on hold for now. We need to talk about how to handle Loki. I'm hoping to turn that matter to an expert on him and Fenrir."

The prez blinked a few times in disbelief. "You're asking someone else?"

Azazel nodded. "Yeah, I know someone who's pretty well-versed on them. So I'm having him give us a few pointers."

Raising my hand, I inquired, "Uh, who, exactly?"

"One of the Five Great Dragon Kings, the Sleeping Dragon, Midgardsormr."

A Dragon King. But what did they have to do with anything?

"Midgardsormr is the obvious choice, but what makes you think he'll respond to you?" Vali asked.

"We'll use the combined powers of the Two Heavenly Dragons and the Dragon Kings Fafnir, Vritra, and Tannin to open the Dragon Gate. Doing so, we can summon Midgardsormr's consciousness while keeping his body dormant in the depths of the seas of northern Europe."

I had no idea anything like that was even possible. Legendary dragons were full of surprises.

"D-does that mean…you need me, too…? To be honest, I feel like I'm surrounded by monsters here…," Saji said timidly.

His Sacred Gear housed the dragon Vritra.

"Well, you'll be one of the essential elements to making it work. You can leave most of the effort to the Two Heavenly Dragons and me, however. For now, just wait until I get in touch with Tannin. And

I'll need to discuss potential countermeasures with Shemhazai, too. Please wait here on standby, everyone. Baraqiel, let's go."

"Very well."

With that, the two fallen angels promptly left the meeting hall.

Now it was just the Occult Research Club, the student council—and the members of Team Vali.

"Red Dragon Emperor!" Bikou raised his hand.

"Wh-what?" I asked nervously.

Bikou flashed me a mischievous grin. "Can I use the pool downstairs?"

That question had come so far out of left field that I had no idea how to respond.

The prez took a step forward, pointing at Bikou. "Hey. This house belongs to me and Issei Hyoudou, the Red Dragon Emperor. I won't permit you to use it however you please."

It sounded like my home was shared property with her now... Well, selfish remarks like that weren't entirely new for the prez. Not letting Bikou use a pool was seriously mistrustful, but I couldn't blame her. He was affiliated with an enemy organization.

"Come on, what's the problem, Switch Princess—?"

Smack!

The prez slapped Bikou in the face! The sound of it echoed through the room!

Bikou stared back at her, his eyes welling up with tears. "Owwwww! What was that for, Switch Princess?!"

"You! All because of you...! Everywhere I go in the underworld, people are calling me all sorts of weird names!" The prez was furious and on the verge of tears. She was literally shaking with rage.

Clearly, Rias wasn't too pleased about her new moniker. Now that I thought about it, Bikou had been the first person to call her by that name, and now Azazel was using it all the time as well.

"It's fine, isn't it? I've been watching *Breast Dragon*, too, you know? I'm honored that they used the term I invented." Bikou let out an amused chortle. It looked like he truly did enjoy it.

"Nghhhhh! Am I truly expected to continue suffering this insult...?!" The prez, on the other hand, clearly found Bikou's attitude intolerable and was trembling with fury. Her crimson aura was already fanning dangerously.

"S-so this is the final lost Excalibur! Wow! It's amazing!"

"Indeed. Vali uncovered some vital clues through his personal connections, and when we compared that information with the records kept by my family, we were able to uncover it. The precise location must remain a secret, however."

Across the room, Irina and Arthur were discussing the latter's Excalibur. Irina's buoyant personality could be quite useful at times like this. She had a way of getting along with people.

Nearby, Kiba and Xenovia were listening cautiously.

As they were both swordfighters, they were naturally wary of this legendary Holy Sword.

Asia tugged my shirt. She was all but squirming in hesitation.

"What is it, Asia?"

"U-um..." She turned her gaze...toward Vali.

I realized at once what she was asking. "You want to go thank him?"

She nodded silently in the affirmative.

Recently, Vali had rescued Asia when she had found herself hurled into the dimensional void. She probably wanted me to thank him on her behalf for the deed.

Ah, Asia! You're such a good, honest young woman! My pride and joy!

As dangerous as Vali might be, I couldn't refuse the request. After taking Asia's hand, I approached the person in question. Vali was still in his seat, his legs crossed, as he read a complex-looking book.

"Vali. Can we have a moment?"

"What is it, Issei Hyoudou?"

With a little urging, Asia stepped toward him. "U-um... Thank you for saving me the other day."

"Hmm? Ah. Right. I only did it on a whim. Let's not worry about it." Once he finished speaking, Vali's gaze returned to his book at once.

That was probably enough. I tugged on Asia's hand, retreating to a safe distance from that bastard. There was no way I'd ever see eye to eye with him.

Huh?

While I was leading Asia away from Vali, another pair of individuals caught my attention.

"…"

"…*Meow.*"

It was Koneko and Kuroka.

The former was on high alert, glaring across at her sister, who looked content to wear a soft, bewitching smile.

"…K-Koneko's sister is beautiful…but she's also s-s-so scary…" Gasper was trembling behind Koneko's back.

Hey, Gasper! Don't hide behind a girl like that!

Was Kuroka trying to bully Koneko again? I approached the two, putting myself between them.

"I won't let you take Koneko," I said to Kuroka point-blank.

Koneko grabbed my hand and quickly slinked behind my back. She still didn't like being around her sister. I would have to protect her.

Kuroka wore a puzzled look for a few seconds before beaming mischievously at me. Her gaze all but threatened to bore straight through me.

"Oh? Your face has gotten so manly since I last saw you. Is that what happens when you unlock your Balance Breaker? Or have you learned the pleasures of a woman? *Meow.*"

That wink of hers as she finished with a cat sound was undeniably cute. I suppose any sibling of Koneko's had to be attractive.

Still, I couldn't afford to forget that she was a living embodiment of malice and ill intent.

A part of me had to wonder if Koneko would be this enrapturing in a few years' time, however. If so, she would be a serious beauty! I couldn't wait to see it!

No, such lecherous thoughts had to wait until later!

I shook my head! I had to be ready to throw my life on the line if I needed to protect Koneko.

Lap.

—!

I took a step backward. A soft, wet sensation had slid across my cheek.

Then I realized that Kuroka had her tongue peeking seductively from her mouth!

"Hmm. But you still taste like a virgin to me-*ow*."

"W-well, I'm sorry about that!"

I couldn't help responding with anger. I mean, she had been right on the mark!

Hold on, could she tell as much by taste…? That *nekomata* sage magic of hers wasn't to be underestimated!

"Hey, hey. Can you do something for me-*ow*?"

"What…?"

"Make a baby with me-*ow*."

"…Huh?"

I was completely taken aback.

Wh-what did she just say…?

Ignoring my bewilderment, Kuroka explained, "I want a dragon child. A superstrong dragon child. I already asked Vali, but he refused. You're the only one left. Dragons in human form are so rare, but the genes of one of the Two Heavenly Dragons will be more than enough. I want to leave behind a child. So I need a gene donor like you."

…

What on earth was she saying…? M-m-*my* child…?

Xenovia had requested practically the same thing. Kuroka clearly possessed some ulterior motive, however.

Are the genes of a Heavenly Dragon really so enticing? I guess I am a legendary dragon. Maybe I can use that fact to help start my harem?

I thought about it for a moment but just couldn't picture it! If there was actually a market for that, then maybe I could start selling my

genes on the side? It might make a good business. The more I considered it, the more it felt like a troubling notion, though.

"Heh-heh-heh, this is a bargain, no? I'll let you sleep with me-*ow* until we make a baby," Kuroka continued.

I very nearly accepted the offer on the spot, but I could feel the stern glare of the petite girl behind me sending shivers down my spine, so I kept my mouth shut.

Kuroka broke out into a fit of laughter at Koneko's reaction.

"…I won't let you have Issei's…"

I hadn't been able to make out the second half of that sentence, but judging by Kuroka's reaction, she had.

She flashed us both an amused grin and, with a wave of her hand, crossed the room to sit near Vali.

From her spot in a corner of the room, Akeno let out a sigh. She had been acting that way ever since Baraqiel had joined us. Was she really okay with this joint operation?

"You cursed monkey! I'll destroy you!"

"Come at me, Switch Princess!"

Ah. The prez and Bikou are fighting again.

Once Azazel returned, he, Vali, Saji, and I used a teleportation circle to jump to a new destination.

This was all part of our plan to summon a Dragon King. Apparently, it wouldn't work unless we were in a specially prepared location.

We arrived in an empty white space. Was this one of those artificial planes used to host Rating Games? I glanced around, but there was absolutely nothing to see…except for the huge dragon waiting for us, that was.

"I haven't seen you all in days," he joked.

"Tannin!"

Yep, it was my old training mentor. Azazel had said we would need his help in summoning Mid-whatever-his-name-was.

"...So that one is Vritra?" The giant dragon was staring down at the now-trembling Saji.

"A D-D-Dragon...King! An ultimate-class demon...!"

His feelings, it seemed, were a mix of terror and admiration.

"Quit worrying," I assured my comrade in virginity. "The old lizard might look intimidating on the outside, but he's a good guy."

"I-idiot! You can't call him that! This is Tannin the ultimate-class demon we're talking about!"

Seriously, Saji...? I mean, sure, he was amazing, but wasn't this a little too much?

Saji jabbed his finger at me. "Only the greatest of demons are chosen to be elevated to the ultimate class. Heck, everyone in the Rating Game top ten is an ultimate-class demon. Reaching that level means contributions to the underworld, spectacular performances in Rating Games, and unmatched natural abilities. It's the greatest honor and highest ranking there is!" Saji explained enthusiastically.

So Tannin was that great, was he?

An ultimate-class demon. I wanted to aim for those heights, too. Unfortunately, contributing to the underworld was really only possible when you had your own territory there. This would be a long, steep road.

"White Dragon Emperor. I will rip you apart at the first sign of trouble." Tannin glared at Vali, who merely flashed the huge dragon a smirk.

Azazel began the incantation without delay, drawing a special magic circle on the ground. As light ran through those lines, it formed a unique pattern.

"But are you sure he'll come? I've only ever met him two or three times myself," Tannin commented with a sigh.

"So long as the Two Heavenly Dragons are here, he'll have to respond, whether he likes it or not," Azazel answered as he added more to the magic circle.

"Is he a fussy old dragon?" I asked.

Azazel squinted in response. "Basically, he never moves. He's the kind of creature whose awakening is said to signal the end of the world. He doesn't wake up unless he needs to take action. He has surfaced out in the world a couple of times, but he was still slumbering during every instance. A few hundred years ago, he finally declared that he would await the world's end at the bottom of the ocean."

A-and he's a Dragon King...? Just what was the standard used to qualify for that position?

Now I got why he was so hard to contact, at least. Meeting someone at the bottom of the ocean was almost impossible.

"The magic circle is ready. Now then, everyone. Stand in your designated places."

At Azazel's urging, we all took position around the strange magic circle.

Apparently, the design used in the array was supposed to represent the Two Heavenly Dragons and the various Dragon Kings.

Once we were all prepared, Azazel made some final adjustments with the miniature magic circle he was holding in his hand.

Flash.

A faint glow ran through the lines at our feet. The area closest to me glowed red, while that around Vali shone white. Azazel's area was golden, while Saji's was black, and Tannin's was purple.

"The shades reflect the characteristics of each dragon," Ddraig explained. *"They aren't here with us right now, but just so you know, Tiamat is blue, and Yulong, green."*

Huh. To be honest, I didn't really get what the colors had to do with anything.

The magic circle activated. Nonetheless, there was no response, and so we maintained our positions for the next few minutes.

...Was Mid-whatever-his-name-was truly going to show himself? Or his consciousness, at least?

Just as I began to wonder if our efforts were for nothing, something began to seep out from the magic circle—a stereoscopic projection appearing above us.

My jaw dropped as the scale of that image kept on expanding. Saji was just as shocked as I was.

And then—

A gigantic monster towered above us, filling the entirety of this empty space!

He was enormous! Huuuuuge!

There was no doubt about it. He was even bigger than the Great Red! This dragon resembled a gigantic serpent. His head was the same shape as Tannin's, but his coiled body must have been impossibly long.

So he's a long, slender dragon, then? Wait, I heard something about there being two types of dragons in the world, Western-type ones like Tannin and thin, elongated Eastern-type ones.

My shock must have been written plain for all to see, as Tannin began to explain: "Midgardsormr is the largest of our kind. Probably around five or six times the size of the Great Red."

Th-that would make him five or six hundred meters long, right…? That was more massive than any monster I had ever even imagined!

A loud, uncanny noise filled my ears, only adding to my trepidation.

"*…Zzzzzzzzz… Zzzzzzzzz…*"

…Is he snoring? He's asleep?

"As I thought, he slumbers. Hey, wake up, Midgardsormr!" Tannin called out.

Only then did the huge monster open his eyes. "*…I've felt this pulse before. A dragon. Ahhhhh…*"

He let out a huge yawn. His mouth was just as enormous as the rest of him! He could have swallowed Tannin whole!

"*Ah, Tannin? How long has it been?*" he asked leisurely.

Midgard…sormr…right? He glanced around at each of us in turn.

"*…Ddraig and Albion, too… Fafnir…and Vritra…? Oh? Is the world ending already?*"

"No, that isn't it. We called you because we need to ask you something," Tannin responded, and yet—

"*…Zzzzzzzzz…*"

Midgardsormr started snoring all over again! No way! He had fallen asleep in the middle of a conversation?!

"Wake up! You and Yulong were always this indolent. I won't stand for it!" Tannin was mad now.

Midgardsormr opened his huge eyes once more. *"...And you were always quick to anger, Tannin... What do you wish to inquire about?"*

"It's about your brother and father," Tannin stated.

"...His brother and father? Th-that's why we're here? What about Loki and Fenrir?" I turned to Azazel, confused.

"Midgardsormr was originally created by Loki. He might possess enormous power, but with his huge body and legendary lethargy, not even the Norse gods knew what to do with him. They encouraged him to sleep to his heart's content under the sea, so long as he promised to rouse himself at the world's end."

"I—I guess that explains his aliases, the Sleeping Dragon and the Dragon of the End... He must really love dozing..."

"Daddy and Bowwow?" Midgardsormr replied. *"I don't mind. I don't much care for either of them anyway... Ah, but Tannin. Let me confirm something."*

"What?"

"Are Ddraig and Albion not going to fight?"

That massive serpent's equally huge eyes were fixed on Vali and me.

Tannin snorted. "No, they aren't. They've joined forces to defeat Loki and Fenrir."

Midgardsormr seemed to find that prospect amusing, his maw curling in a grin. *"Oh? Interesting... I was wondering why they were standing so casually next to each other,"* he said before turning back to the topic at hand. *"Bowwow will be more trouble than Daddy. Few survive an encounter with those fangs. But he does have a weakness. The dwarven chain Gleipnir is strong enough to bind him. With that, you'll be able to keep him at bay."*

Bowwow, huh? Well, from Midgardsormr's point of view, Fenrir must have been like a miniature puppy.

"We've already looked into that. Unfortunately, our information from the Norse pantheon suggests that Gleipnir didn't work last time. I was hoping you could share another strategy," Tannin responded.

Hmm. I was having a hard time keeping up with the two dragons. But so long as the others knew what was going on, I suppose that didn't matter.

"I see... Perhaps Daddy enhanced Bowwow, then? If so, you should seek out the dark elves of northern Europe. Their elders should know how to reinforce the magic of dwarven artifacts. I'll transmit the location of the elves to Ddraig's and Albion's Sacred Gears."

Azazel pointed toward Vali. "Send it to the White Dragon Emperor. We'll have a hard time getting it out of the other one. His mind isn't all there."

Well, sorry for being such an idiot!

Insulted though I was, I couldn't help but whisper, "So elves and dwarves really do exist..."

I mean, I had only ever heard of those kinds of beings in fantasy novels and movies. Then again, if angels and demons could exist, it didn't seem too far-fetched.

"They've mostly withdrawn into alternate dimensions to escape environmental changes, but some continue to reside in a few distant corners of the world."

Vali, having received the information, spoke up. "I have it. Azazel, activate a projection of the globe."

Azazel pulled out his phone and displayed a three-dimensional map of the world. Vali pointed to an area on the map, and Azazel immediately sent that location to the others waiting back at home.

"...Ha. You're full of information, I see," Tannin remarked to Midgardsormr with obvious admiration.

"Well, the elves and dwarves take care of me when I go up to the surface."

Wouldn't it be a major incident if this guy rose up from the sea? He was simply too huge.

Now that we knew how to tackle our first problem, Tannin moved on to the next. "What about Loki?"

"Mjölnir might work against Daddy."

Azazel cupped his chin in his hand. "In other words, we'll still have to attack him head-on? I wonder if the Norse thunder god Thor will be willing to part with Mjölnir if Odin asks him for it..."

"I doubt he'll offer it readily. Only gods are capable of wielding weapons like that," Vali pointed out.

"In that case, try asking the dwarves or the dark elves. They should be holding on to Odin's Mjölnir replica."

"You're a wellspring of knowledge, huh? Thanks, Midgardsormr," Azazel said with clear gratitude.

"No, no. It's fun to chat every once in a while. But it's time. I need to sleep. Fuahhhhh..."

Midgardsormr let out another massive yawn as the projection began to fade away.

"I owe you my thanks, too," Tannin added.

Midgardsormr's maw twisted into a contented grin. *"Don't worry about it. Wake me up if something big happens."*

With those parting words, the projection faded away entirely.

Midgardsormr. He was one weird Dragon King. Would I ever meet him again?

And so, having received the information we needed, we set to action.

–O●O–

After breakfast the next morning, everyone gathered in the underground hall again. The Gremory and Sitri Familias were skipping school today. However, we were sending familiars disguised as ourselves to keep up appearances.

Our decisive confrontation with Loki was fast approaching, so we all needed to take a break to prepare. Nonetheless, those Familia members who were looking forward to school were dejected. All of us liked going to Kuou Academy. I loved it there!

Chairwoman Sona seemed particularly frustrated that she couldn't go. Perhaps because so many responsibilities fell on her as student council chairwoman. She had to be fretting something would go awry in her absence.

Azazel, grumbling under his breath, entered the room. His expression looked unusually sour.

"I come with a present from that good-for-nothing old geezer Odin. It's the replica of Mjölnir. He really did go and hide it in the middle of nowhere. How the hell did Midgardsormr know about it...?"

"Is it that incredible?" I asked.

"It's a replica of the hammer used by the Norse thunder god, Thor," Azazel explained. "It's filled with divine lightning."

That did sound impressive.

"Yes, Lord Odin is willing to lend you this replica of the Mjölnir, Red Dragon Emperor. Here you go," Rossweisse stated before presenting me with...a totally average-looking hammer.

Huh? This is it?

It looked like the kind of tool an everyday carpenter might use. Excluding a bit of fancy engraving on it, there was nothing that set it apart.

"Direct your aura through it."

As Rossweisse instructed, I focused my demonic powers on the hammer.

There was a sudden flash of light, and the hammer abruptly increased in size!

Thud!

The Mjölnir replica grew taller than I was and slammed hard into the ground.

The whole building shuddered at the force of the impact. It was so heavy that its weight had smashed through the floor.

Nghhhhh!

I tried as hard as I could to lift the hammer back up, yet it wouldn't budge. It was just too heavy! Maybe I could do it in my Balance Breaker state? Even then, I wasn't certain I could swing it around with any degree of control…

"Hey, hey, hey! You poured too much power into it. Tone it down," Azazel scolded with a sigh.

When I decreased my aura as instructed, the Mjölnir replica shrank back to a manageable size, until it was a perfect fit for my hands.

…But it was still too heavy! Try as I might, it refused to yield!

After watching me struggle for a bit, Azazel explained, "You should be able to lift it if you activate your Balance Breaker. For now, just let go."

I released the hammer as ordered and watched as it returned to its original size.

"It may be a replica, but it's almost as strong as the real thing. Normally, only a god would be able to wield it, but with some help from Baraqiel, I've modified it so that demons can hold it, too. Don't swing it around too carelessly, got it? The high-energy lightning stored in that thing could lay waste to this whole area."

"Seriously?! Whoa! That's terrifying!"

I shrank back in fear at Teach's warning. Why was he giving such a dangerous weapon to *me*?

Ah, but if I transfer my boosted power into it… That might be enough to defeat Loki.

"Vali, why don't you go see that old clod, Odin? He might have something special for you, too," Azazel remarked with evident amusement.

Please, Teach, stop! I pleaded silently. My rival was already strong enough! At this rate, he would be unstoppable!

Surprisingly, Vali shook his head in refusal. "No need. I'm planning to master this Heavenly Dragon's original power. I don't need any extra equipment. No, what I seek is something else."

That declaration really struck something with me. Vali had an abundance of innate talent. His abilities were more than strong enough, even without putting inordinate amounts of effort into training or acquiring new techniques like I had to.

I was told that I would never surpass him in terms of demonic power or abilities. Even Vali's physical prowess came to him naturally, while I needed to practice constantly just to maintain mine.

It was beyond frustrating.

The stats of my supposedly fated rival far eclipsed my own.

No, I reminded myself. I still had room for growth. One of these days, I would find a new path to greatness and defeat him. I had to.

I couldn't give up. One of these days, I would definitely—

"Oh, Bikou. I've got a message for you, too," Azazel remarked offhandedly, turning to face the descendant of Sun Wukong.

"Huh? For me?" he questioned, pointing to his own face in bewilderment. "Who from?"

"I'll read it out. 'You blighted fool. You're in for a good disciplining when I find you.' It's signed 'The First.' Sounds like he's out searching for you with Yulong."

Sweat plastered Bikou's forehead, his face turning pale. "G-Gramps... He must have realized I've teamed up with terrorists. And Yulong, too!"

Given Bikou's usual cheerful spirit, I would never have expected to see him looking so panicked.

Huh? "The First"? D-does that mean the original Sun Wukong, by any chance...?

"Bikou, should we drop in on your hometown? It should be interesting meeting the first Sun Wukong and the great Yulong."

"...Cut it out, Vali. I thought Yulong was supposed to be retired, but even putting him aside, my gramps is a real monster. And he's still active. The level of his sage and beast magic is seriously off the charts..."

This guy had thrown himself into battle against Tannin, but he was visibly terrified of his predecessor...

Speaking of which, Tannin would apparently be joining us on the day of the battle with Loki and was waiting on standby down in the underworld. For that, at least, I felt reassured. He would be fighting alongside us!

Azazel cleared his throat before addressing us all. "Let's go over our strategy. First, we'll wait for Loki to appear at the meeting place. Once he arrives, the Sitri Familia will transport him and Fenrir to a safer location, an abandoned quarry. It's a wide-open area and durable enough to survive a decent rampage. Issei and Vali, our Two Heavenly Dragons, will be pivotal to our counterstrategy, taking on Loki. Our other members—the Gremory Familia, along with Team Vali—will deal with Fenrir. Your job is to use the Gleipnir to bind him. Whatever happens, you have to make sure Fenrir can't get to Odin. That creature's fangs can destroy a god. Not even the chief god of the Norse pantheon will survive them. We have to prevent that at any cost."

That was our battle plan. The Sitri Familia would transfer our enemies and us to a safe location, where Vali and I would fight Loki together while the others tried to ensnare Fenrir.

…There was a lot of pressure being put on us all here. My opponent was a real-life god… Even with me fighting alongside Vali, there was no guarantee this would end well…

I suppose we didn't have much choice, though. A confrontation with a god… You really never knew what life was going to throw at you.

"All right. We left the chain with the dark elf elders, so we'll just have to wait for them to finish it. All that's left…is Saji."

"What is it, Mr. Azazel?"

"You're essential to this strategy. Vritra is contained in your Sacred Gear, after all."

Saji was so shocked being called out like this that his eyes all but popped out of their sockets. "H-hold on! I—I don't have any crazy powers like Hyoudou or the White Dragon Emperor! I can't take on a god or that Fenrir! I—I thought we would all just be transferring everyone else to the battlefield!"

Saji couldn't hide his dismay. His abilities could certainly be effective, but I had to admit that he would still have a hard time facing Loki or Fenrir.

Azazel was undoubtedly aware of that, too, and merely breathed a sigh. "I'm not telling you to fight on the front line. But I *do* want you to support everyone with Vritra's powers. Issei and Vali, in particular, will be counting on you."

"S-support them?"

"You're going to need a little extra training, however. There's something I want to try. Sona, I'm going to borrow him for a little while," Teach declared to the chairwoman.

"Very well. But where will you be taking him?"

"The fallen angel territory in the underworld. To the Grigori Research Institute," Azazel said with a grin.

Ah, I knew that face. Saji was in for some hellish practice.

Speaking from experience, when Azazel got this excited, someone was undoubtedly about to be subjected to true hell. I may have only known him for a few months, but I had come to understand that part of him only too well.

"Saji. Teach's training is fiendish. I almost died from the regimen he planned for me. And *you're* going to a *research institute*. I hope you've prepared a will." I patted my friend on the shoulder, flashing him a look of pity and consolation.

My words only served to amplify poor Saji's worry.

"Ha-ha-ha! All right, then. Let's go." Azazel grabbed Saji by the collar and activated a magic circle.

"Seriously?! H-help meeeee! Hyoudooooouuuuu! Chairwomaaaaan!"

The magic circle burst into light, enveloping the weeping Saji.

Farewell, my friend. We won't ever forget you!

I had to wonder how he'd be able to assist Vali and me, though. Just what was Azazel thinking…?

"Vritra lay dormant within that youth until his battle with you. That must have something to do with it," Ddraig said.

If that was true, then I was looking forward to seeing what Saji was capable of.

"By the way, Ddraig. Aren't you going to talk to Albion?" I inquired.

This was a rare reunion for the two dragons. Surely, they must have had a lot to talk about.

"No, there's nothing to discuss. Is there, White?" This time, Ddraig spoke out loud so that everyone could hear him.

"...Don't speak to me. No so-called Breast Dragon Emperor is worthy of being my nemesis."

Albion's reaction was beyond cold!

"W-wait! D-don't misunderstand! It's my host, Issei Hyoudou, who people are calling that!" Ddraig cried back, trying to defend himself.

Hey! Don't put all this on me!

Admittedly, this kind of *was* my fault...

"...Using b-b-breasts to awaken and deactivate your Juggernaut Drive... I felt like weeping when I saw the depths to which you have been reduced, Red." Albion's voice was heavy with disappointment.

Ddraig broke down into tears. *"I cried, too! I couldn't stop! Waughhhhh!"*

"Ngh. How could this have happened...? We, the proud and noble Heavenly Dragons... Do you realize how saddened I was to see my rival reduced to the level of a children's television hero? Breast Dragon indeed..."

What was going on here...? These legendary dragons, the Two Heavenly Dragons...were both distraught.

Vali seemed just as troubled by the unusual scene.

"...Albion, are you crying again? You wept back when we watched that children's show modeled on Issei Hyoudou, too."

He did? I'd made both Heavenly Dragons sob?

Vali turned to me, his face clouded. "Sorry about this, Issei Hyoudou. I don't suppose you know how to comfort them when they get like this?"

"How would I?! Anyway, I'm sorry about being a Breast Dragon, okay?!"

Ugh! What was I supposed to do?

While I dealt with this odd situation, everyone else continued with the arrangements for our upcoming confrontation with Loki.

–O●O–

Everyone set about their preparations. The prez and I were in my room, trying to work out how to use the Mjölnir.

We hadn't gotten too far into it when a magic circle appeared in the center of the floor, from which a silver-haired maid emerged.

It was Grayfia, carrying what looked like a pile of documents.

"Lady Rias. I've brought the information relating to Gleipnir. The enchanted chain will be delivered directly to the battlefield on the day of the confrontation."

"Thank you, Grayfia." The prez accepted the papers and began to leaf through them.

Now that both the prez and Grayfia were here, a certain question came to mind.

"U-um," I began, my voice faltering. "Seeing as you're both here, there's something I want to ask…"

Grayfia turned her cool eyes toward me. She was Sirzechs's Queen and his wife. On top of that, she was Millicas's mother.

"What is it?" she pressed.

"…U-um…"

I was a little unsure how to put this, but I decided to bite the bullet. "It's about Akeno. Why doesn't she get along with her dad? I mean, Baraqiel doesn't seem so bad to me…"

Grayfia and the prez exchanged glances.

After a brief silence, the prez chose to speak up. "…She has bitter memories."

Akeno's mother had been a shrine maiden at a famous Japanese temple.

Her name was Shuri Himejima. Akeno had elected to take her mother's surname.

One day, Baraqiel, having been gravely wounded in an encounter with enemy forces, appeared near the temple. Akeno's mother saved the wounded fallen angel leader, nursing him back to health.

"Akeno Himejima's mother established a close relationship with Baraqiel, and before long, she was pregnant," Grayfia explained.

The prez took over from there. "Baraqiel couldn't leave Akeno or her mother behind, and so he stayed nearby while continuing his work as a fallen angel leader remotely. They had a quiet and peaceful life. However..."

That happiness didn't last.

Akeno's mother's relatives misunderstood the situation, thinking that the black-winged fallen angel had robbed her of her free will, and so they called on several famous shamanistic practitioners.

Baraqiel didn't have much trouble driving the shamans away. Nonetheless, having been so soundly defeated, there were some among them who wanted revenge.

"They informed the enemies of the fallen angels of Baraqiel's location," Grayfia said.

There was a sorrowful cast to the prez's eyes. "It all came down to bad luck. Baraqiel just happened to be out that day. His enemies attacked Akeno and her mother without hesitation. By the time Baraqiel realized the danger and returned...Akeno's mother had already died protecting her daughter..."

The attack had drilled into Akeno just how much her father, as a fallen angel leader, was despised by his enemies, and they drove that point home by murdering her mother in front of her very eyes.

"Since that day, Akeno Himejima has borne a resoundingly negative view of fallen angels. And of course, she still resents her mother's murder and closed her heart to Lord Baraqiel."

Grayfia's explanation left me speechless. I had never expected anything so extreme.

A few years afterward, Akeno, being half fallen angel herself, was driven away by her family. She wandered, alone, with no home to call her own until she met the prez.

"But you know, Issei? When Akeno joined my Familia, she found a new purpose as a demon. She was happier. And after meeting you, her attitude toward fallen angels has softened… I think she understands, deep down, that there was nothing that could have been done to save her mother, but she isn't strong enough to accept that just yet."

"…It was my fault."

After learning what had happened to Akeno, I decided to ask Azazel, who was still in the VIP room on the top floor, about it.

He recounted the tragedy from his perspective, surprisingly taking the blame for it all.

"I was the one who called him that day. I had a job I couldn't pull off without him. So I summoned him away without thinking. And while he was gone…his wife was murdered."

"…Teach. Is that why you've been trying to look out for Akeno all this time?"

…Azazel fell silent, his hands still busy at his work. At that moment, another figure entered the room.

"Azazel. I'm back." It was Vali.

"Oh. It's you. How did it go?"

Vali extended his hand, creating a small magic circle above his palm. *That symbol…* It looked like the kind of emblem featured in the magic circles the Norse gods used.

"I learned a fair amount of Norse magic. I should be able to counter Loki's attacks, at least to some extent," Vali stated. In his other hand, he was holding the same book I had seen him reading earlier.

Was he seriously studying Norse magic to fight Loki? And he learned it in such a short period of time...?

He must have had serious magic talent. There was no way I could have picked up any new skills so swiftly...

Azazel nodded in confirmation. "Good... All right, I'm just about finished here, too, so I guess it's time to take a break."

Leaving Vali and me behind, Azazel exited the room.

Without Teach in the room, an eerie tension filled the chamber. Vali sat down on a nearby sofa and went back to reading his book, while I settled into a seat a reasonable distance away from him.

Whenever he wasn't needed, Vali had a habit of disappearing with Bikou. I didn't think he liked staying in my house longer than necessary. I guessed that he didn't want to get overly familiar with us. Then again, the same went for me, too.

I also wanted to leave, but for some reason, I found myself overcome with a sudden urge to try to talk to him a little.

No decent topics came to mind, but after a little head-scratching, I opened my mouth. "...He might be an evil one, but still, I never would have expected to fight a real-life god..."

I hadn't anticipated a response from Vali, but to my surprise, without lifting his gaze from his book, he answered, "You should keep this in mind. There are good gods and bad ones. And depending on your point of view, the former can still seem like the latter..."

"A bad god... Why doesn't he want peace? I'm a demon, but all I want to do is live normally and have fun with the prez and the others day in, day out."

Vali closed his book there, turning his gaze up at me. "Your *peace* is excruciating for some people."

Excruciating...?

Did that mean one's standard for enjoying life could be different depending on their situation...? If so, that was an unhappy thought. I didn't want to get dragged into a war.

Hmm… If only everyone understood the splendor of breasts, maybe we could all live in tranquility…

"Is the world painful for you, too?" I inquired.

Vali stared up at the ceiling. "It's just boring. Which is why I'm looking forward to this joint operation. It's going to be fun." His grin was so broad that it sent a shiver down my spine.

He really was a battle maniac, the kind of person who lived to fight…

"I'm not. There are too many super-powerful enemies out there."

"But *that's* what makes the world so fascinating. I'm going to become stronger than anyone."

So that was Vali's dream, was it? He might have been a Heavenly Dragon like me, but we had vastly different goals.

"I… I'll be happy to be the mightiest of Pawns and to get promoted to a high-class demon. Then I'll make my own harem."

Admittedly, becoming an ultimate-class demon didn't sound too bad, either, but it seemed like you needed to achieve something reputable with your underworld territory first. Or maybe I could build a massive business empire off this whole Breast Dragon thing…?

Damnit! What am I supposed to do? My dreams keep ballooning!

"That certainly sounds like you," Vali commented, still smiling.

"Oh, and I have one other goal."

Yep, I had almost forgotten the most important one.

I stared directly toward Vali as I declared, "I'm going to overcome you."

At this, Vali's expression shifted to one of purest joy, something I had never seen on him before. "Yeah, I'll be waiting. I'll be happy, too, to see you get stronger. I was disappointed when I first met you. You were the weakest of all Red Dragon Emperors. Yet lately, you've been growing in an entirely new direction. You're probably the first Red Dragon Emperor capable of using those powers while also being able to communicate with Ddraig."

Is that true, partner?

"It is. Didn't I already tell you? You're the first of my hosts in all of

history to communicate with me this much. And you haven't allowed yourself to drown in my powers or surrender yourself to overconfidence."

Ddraig paused there, leaving Vali to elaborate. "Each of those hosts wielded that incredible, destructive power purely as they liked. And in the end, they were overwhelmed by it, perishing in battle."

"*You may be the least talented Red Dragon Emperor to have ever lived, the weakest in terms of power and every other measure. And yet—*"

"You're the first Red Dragon Emperor to actually learn how to properly use that strength."

I could feel my cheeks flushing with embarrassment at Ddraig's and Vali's words. Was it just me, or did they have higher expectations for me than I did of myself? That was intimidating in its own way.

Even Albion offered his thoughts. "*Hosts like that are always the most bothersome. They don't leave many openings when the time comes to do battle.*"

Vali nodded. "That's right. I had an interesting thought just now. It might be fun to have a team battle, something like a Rating Game, between the two of us one day."

A Rating Game between Vali's group and mine?

…*Yeah. Yeah. Yeah! That* does *sound like fun.*

I wasn't entirely sure why, but part of me was really looking forward to such a match.

"Eh… That sounds good! I'm going to build the strongest Familia out there! Filled with beautiful girls and women!"

"Ha-ha-ha. I'll look forward to it. But I might need to fight against the Gremory Familia first… Let's defeat each other someday."

"Rias Gremory's Familia won't lose to you easily! But you had better not try to attack in some underhanded terrorist way!"

"Heh. I can't promise that."

There was no telling when that day would come.

However, I wanted, more than I could possibly have imagined, to defeat Vali…

"Ahhh, the spirit of youth."

Whoa!

Old man Odin had appeared entirely out of nowhere. Had he already finished all his work?

He looked to be deeply moved by my exchange with Vali.

"This generation's Red and White are unique. You used to do nothing more than rampage, turning any situation into a direct confrontation, destroying everything around you, and then kicking the bucket. You both resorted to your Juggernaut Drives whenever you felt like it. I wonder how many mountains and islands you eradicated?" The old man let out a sigh.

Rossweisse, who had appeared behind Odin, added, "That one is an obscene dragon, and the other a terrorist, yet they're surprisingly calm. When I first met them, I was sure they would break into an immediate battle. But now look at them both."

Well, forgive me for being so obscene!

But maybe Vali and I really were rare, at least for hosts of Heavenly Dragons. Just what was so different about our predecessors and us, though? Ah, maybe that could have something to do with helping me find a way to resolve the lingering regrets in the Boosted Gear?

"Incidentally, White Dragon Emperor... Which part do you like most?" Odin asked Vali with a lecherous smirk.

...Were the two of them about to start talking about something pervy?

"Which part of what exactly?" Vali questioned back, tilting his head to one side inquisitively.

At that moment, the old geezer pointed first to Rossweisse's breasts, then her buttocks, then her thighs. "Which part of a woman's body. Our Red Dragon Emperor here is big on tits. I thought you might have a similar obsession."

"Out of the question. I'm not a *Breast Dragon*," Vali responded, clearly mortified.

Sorry again! This is all my fault!

"Now, now. You're a man. There must be some part you like, isn't there?"

"…I don't put a lot of thought into that kind of thing. If you're going to make me choose, the hips, maybe," Vali responded offhandedly. "If you ask me, the line from the waist to the hip perfectly symbolizes a woman's beauty."

"…I see. So you're an Ass Dragon Emperor." No sooner did the lecherous old geezer murmur those words than—

"…N-nghhhhh…"

—Albion began bawling his eyes out.

I turned to Odin. "Stop it. Our Two Heavenly Dragons are going through a delicate phase here!"

How could I not have felt empathetic toward Ddraig and Albion? This could well have been the first issue in their whole lives that had literally shocked them both to tears.

I needed to be more considerate of Ddraig in the future.

"Don't cry, Albion. I'm always here to talk." Even Vali had kind words for his partner!

Everyone! The Two Heavenly Dragons really have entered a delicate phase!

"You poor thing… Maybe someone will write a fairy tale about you one day. 'The Pitiful Dragon.' Hmm."

Odin! Cut it out already!

The old man cleared his throat. "Yep, it's good to be young."

All of a sudden, he sounded like a more dignified elder.

"What do you mean?" I asked.

Odin stroked his beard. "Until the present age, I was convinced that this wrinkled fool could solve anything just by drawing from his big bag of wisdom. But that's just the arrogance of the aged. What matters most are the possibilities that you striplings bring to the table. Oh-ho-ho. I only truly realized that recently. I've been such an idiot… My pride gave birth to Loki. And now, because of my arrogance, you young'uns have to suffer these trials." The old man's eye seemed filled with regret to me. I didn't quite follow his train of thought, however.

"I'm not sure I get it, but shouldn't we just keep moving forward, one step at a time?" I suggested casually.

That was the principle I lived by.

Odin's expression, however, was one of mute shock.

Wh-what's with that dramatic response?

But then he started to chuckle in amusement. "...It's good to be young. Yes, talking to you young'uns sure gets this old blood flowing."

I was still lost, but at least the old man looked happy.

–O●O–

I sat cross-legged in a meditative position in an empty room in my house, dressed in no more than my trousers, with my chest and upper body exposed.

...

I was trying to focus, to bury my consciousness into my Sacred Gear.

Azazel had instructed me to try this. It was all in an attempt to discover new possibilities.

"—. Hahhhhhh..."

Having reached my limit after half an hour, my concentration faltered. I took a deep breath.

It was no good.

With Ddraig's help, I had tried to immerse myself in the Sacred Gear. Yet it was like swimming through pitch darkness, and after passing through it, I came only to a white expanse.

It was filled with tables and chairs, with people who looked like former hosts of the Red Dragon Emperor sitting at each.

They all wore hollow expressions, as though robbed of all awareness. Perhaps I should have expected as much. They were merely residual memories, after all.

According to Ddraig, they regained their full senses of self only when I entered my Juggernaut Drive. When that happened, they would ceaselessly bombard me with curses, all in an effort to make my Juggernaut Drive go out of control.

I tried talking to them one by one…but never got a reaction.

The mental burden of delving this deep into my Sacred Gear was severe, so I couldn't stay there for long. Ultimately, I had to call it a day without achieving anything.

This wasn't going to be easy. Could I really push the powers of the Red Dragon Emperor to the next level just by conversing with all my predecessors?

Either way, I would just have to try meditating patiently again tomorrow. As in everything, persistence was the key to moving forward.

Click…

The door to my room swung open.

I glanced up to see who it was and saw Akeno dressed in a thin white gown.

She had already sucked the accumulated dragon power out of my arm a couple of days ago. We didn't need to do it again so soon.

She closed the door behind her.

Click.

Hold on, did she just lock it?

She was wearing her hair down, and her expression was somehow coquettish.

"…Issei."

"Yes?"

Her voice was small and weak… She approached me slowly, and then—with a rustling of silk, she pulled at the obi holding her gown closed, and let it…!

Plop.

It f-f-f-f-fell to the ground!

Blood gushed down my nose. Akeno was as naked as the day she had been born…!

Her white, exposed body… I-it wasn't just her breasts that I had a full view of!

I went still at this unbelievable development!

B-b-b-b-breasts! And more!

She drew closer to me while I sat paralyzed and wrapped her arms around my neck. And then she embraced me!

Plop. Squeeze.

Her breasts! Her arms! Her thighs! Her whole body! They were all wrapping around me so wonderfully!

My brain overloaded from the soft, exhilaratingly elastic sensation of her feminine flesh!

Ahhhhh... Akeno...

Why was her body so tender, so deliciously soft, so wonderfully silky?!

She was pushing her breasts up against my chest with all her strength! I could feel her nipples against my skin!

I was helpless when faced with the wondrous sensation of a woman. Her glossy velvet hair gave off a sweet scent. Ah, why did girls have to smell so nice?

As her fragrant aroma filled my nostrils, my brain erupted into bloom like a field of flowers!

Then she drew up close to my ear and whispered, "Make love to me."

...

Whaaaaa—?!

My brain stopped for a moment. Once it was working again, I suffered an explosive nosebleed.

...M-m-m-m-make looooove?!

Out of all the phrases I had wanted to hear from a girl, Akeno had just said my absolute number one!

B-but seriously?! Th-th-that is what this means, right?! It is, isn't it?!

Her breasts felt wonderful as she hugged me naked. Her pale skin was so dazzling! I had no idea where to put my hands, and so I left them hanging up in the air!

My first time! Was my first time going to be with Akeno?!

She stared straight into my face, our eyes meeting.

Akeno's expression seemed hollow somehow. Her gaze had a desperate, almost self-destructive cast, as though she didn't care what happened to her.

She drew closer to my face and tried to kiss me.

If I let this become real, I might find myself pushing her down, and we might even go all the way...

This was my chance! Perhaps the greatest, most fortuitous opportunity of my life! And yet... I knew it wasn't right.

I rested my hands on Akeno's shoulders, gingerly moving her away.

The skin beneath my palms felt so supple and wonderful, very nearly destroying my sense of reason.

But I had to endure! I mean, this was wrong!

"...Why? Aren't I attractive enough...?" she asked, voice trembling.

Judging by her reaction, she must have thought I would have embraced her back.

There was nothing to be gained by lying, so my only choice was to tell her the truth!

"N-n-not at all! You're amazing! I could never grow tired of your huge, soft breasts, no matter how many times I touch them! I want to stroke your waist, grab ahold of your butt, squeeze your perfectly proportioned thighs... I want to relish every last part of you and bury my face in your chest!"

"...Then why don't you? I...want you to. I want to give my body to you, and I want you to embrace me in your arms and make everything else go away... You can push past all those things that keep rising up in front of me... Why don't you?"

"Because you look so sad."

"—."

Judging by Akeno's expression, it looked like my statement had snapped her out of whatever was going on.

"When you do something naughty with me, you usually look like you're having fun, Akeno," I elaborated. "But right now, it seems to me that you're doing this to push away sadness."

"...You're right. But does saying that change anything? I'm trying to clear my mind by letting you make love to me, so that I can go into battle free of doubts. I thought curling up in a man's chest would free me from all these negative emotions..."

That was totally wrong! Even if it did help her feel better, it would only be temporary!

That hardly seemed like a genuine solution!

I picked up the gown that Akeno had let fall to the floor and draped it over her body. Then I hugged her softly.

My brain went haywire as her body pressed against mine again, but I forced myself to remain rational.

"...I can hold you like this. W-we don't need to do anything naughty! I—I'm filled with lecherous thoughts! I really want to do it with you, Akeno, but not when you're feeling so awful!"

"...Issei."

Despite knowing about Akeno's past, I was too much of an idiot to come up with anything appropriate to say. Nonetheless, if she was willing to lean on me, I would hold her until she felt safe!

Akeno didn't say anything for a while.

It seemed to me that she'd been grappling with conflicting emotions ever since reuniting with her father. With nowhere else to turn, she must have sought out a false relief in the arms of a man—me.

But that would only scar her even more! It wouldn't do! Akeno would definitely regret it later!

Thus, I reasoned it might be best to simply tell her my true feelings.

Holding Akeno tight, I whispered into her ear, "I'll stay by your side. Whenever you feel sad or lonely, I'll be there to hold you like this. So please. Don't feel down, Akeno."

That was all I could do.

"...I'm such a fool... You are, too, Issei..."

"Probably, but I'll still protect you, Akeno."

"...Issei... Thank you... I love you." Her saddened voice sounded somehow relieved.

We remained hugging each other until Akeno felt well enough to leave.

Akeno. If I'm good enough for you, I'll stick with you forever. So please, find a way to return to your usual cheerful self.

–O●O–

That night, the prez, Asia, and I lay together in bed. Rias and Asia had already fallen asleep, but I was preoccupied with thoughts of Akeno and the upcoming battle.

For one day, a lot had happened. I had spoken to Vali, met a Dragon King, learned about Akeno's past, heard Azazel's thoughts about new possibilities... I was glad I hadn't wounded Akeno any further.

Shudder...

All of a sudden, my body trembled with anxiety.

It was no mystery why. I was scared because the day of the battle was drawing near. We were up against a god. That was terrifying. I wanted to run away and hide. If possible, I didn't want to fight at all. I could very well end up dead.

Obviously, that wasn't an option.

After hearing out Sirzechs, the prez had decided to pursue this course of action. My only choice was to believe in her and push forward.

To protect my friends, to defend the women whom I loved. I would use all my powers to overcome this new trial.

"Can't sleep?"

That was the prez's voice.

I turned around and found her lying there, staring at me.

"...Akeno looked happy earlier. Did something happen?"

Uh-oh. Had Rias noticed?

"W-we didn't do anything naughty!" I blurted out, looking away.

At this reaction, the prez, her eyes half-lidded, pinched my cheek. "I didn't ask you that... You are telling me the truth, though?"

"Y-yes. I'm still a virgin..."

At this, she finally released my cheek. "Good."

Man, the prez sure was strict with her servants.

I stroked my still painful cheek, then she took my hand in her own and began to guide it—through the gap in her negligee and to her breasts!

Squish.

Ah, this was it! The prez's breasts! They were so smooth, so elastic, so huge and soft!

My fingers had never known a more incredible sensation! I had reached the point that whenever I thought about the feeling of boobs, it was always the prez's that sprang to mind!

"U-um… Prez…?" I could feel a trickle of blood leaking from my nose.

"…Your heart is racing, isn't it?" she asked me gently. "Of course it is. We're going to be fighting a god soon. I'm nervous, too."

I could feel Rias's heartbeat through my hand.

"I—I know that. B-but why are you letting me touch your breasts?"

"Heh-heh, you don't remember? When we went to the underworld, I promised to let you touch them, didn't I? And I thought this might be the best way to help you relax. You're so anxious that you can't sleep, aren't you?"

I was no match for her. She was incredible, this Prez of mine.

"You'll be fighting on the front line, an incredibly important position, against a deity. I'm sure you're fretting about it. That's why you're still up, right?"

My great lady knew everything. She had seen right through me.

"…Yes. I'm scared. I'm honored to be given this role, but I'm frightened. Can I really do it? What will happen if I fail…? All this pressure being put on me is nerve-racking."

There I was, doing something I would never have thought to do—blurting out my weaknesses to the prez.

Why? Normally, I would never be able to say this to anyone, but with my hand on her breast, confessing to Rias felt only natural. And it *did* put me at ease.

"It's okay. You can tell me what's on your mind. I love everything about you, Issei. Including your weaknesses."

There was no way I would be able to show this side of myself to Asia or Akeno.

Yet with the prez, I could…

They were so squishy, and holding them was enough to soothe my heart. There was something mysterious about her chest.

Was that because they were the breasts of a loved one? Or because they were my master's?

I couldn't say for certain. But they undoubtedly possessed a special power that relieved my anxieties.

"Maybe it's because I'm the Breast Dragon, but touching them is genuinely relaxing," I confessed.

The prez stroked my cheek. "That's fine. You can be a Breast Dragon. You're my pride and joy, Issei. Be strong. I believe in your dream of becoming the mightiest of Pawns."

"Prez…"

"If my chest comforts you and helps make you stronger, then I'm happy to be your Switch Princess—your private Switch Princess. I couldn't ask for anything more than to be the source of your power, my dear Issei."

The prez's face drew close to mine—until her lips quietly pressed up against my own.

Our third kiss.

It was gentler, deeper, and lasted much longer than the previous ones had…

Prez, for you and the others, I will become as mighty as can be. That's a promise.

Odin

"Yo, Gramps. It's almost time for your conference. We're just about ready over here."

"Azazel…? Hmm."

"What's up? You're looking pretty serious there for once."

"...I'm starting to think that my style of governance has caused quite a few problems not only for my own country, but the young'uns here, too."

"I always hated you Norse guys, holing yourselves up in your Northern wastes with your antiquated ways of thinking. But then you stepped up onto the stage, ready to join us when we reached out in peace and cooperation."

"...I *am* an old clod. But every now and then, I like to see how you striplings think. And when I considered the future of all the young'uns back home, I started wondering if maybe forging a new path wasn't so bad after all."

"Make that dream a reality, Gramps. That's why you came here to see the Japanese gods, right? Sure, you claimed to be sightseeing, but you were really here to learn about their mythological system, weren't you? It was all for the sake of ensuring the talks go well. You can count on us for help."

"Hmm. I don't need you to tell me that... But just for today, maybe I'll be willing to share a drink with you, boyo."

Life.4
The Two Heavenly Dragons vs the Evil God Loki!

"How about a breast-filled maid café?!"

"Denied." The prez rejected my suggestion with a tired sigh.

During our after-school club activities, we were trying to work out what we would do for the Academy Festival. It was a busy time for all of us right now, but it was still best if we decided on an idea sooner rather than later. After all, today was the only day we'd been allowed to attend school until this whole Loki thing was over.

Naturally, I had suggested a maid café! And a breast-themed one, at that! If our Two Great Ladies, Rias and Akeno, took the helm, we would probably become the most popular and successful event at the whole celebration!

"But if we did that, other guys would be able to see the president's and Akeno's chests. You realize that, don't you?"

Kiba's comment left me flabbergasted. He was right! Other guys would be able to visually devour the prez's and Akeno's precious breasts! That wouldn't do at all! *I* was the only one with the right to ogle them!

"...Ugh, you're right. Then I guess a breast-themed haunted house is out of the question as well..."

"...Were you considering that, too, you sick freak?" Koneko was aghast at my next failed suggestion.

As if to hammer home my regret, the prez breathed another heavy exhale. "Look, Issei. A naughty theme like that would certainly help score us points. But the student council, let alone the teaching staff, simply won't allow it."

She was right.

But in that case, what *could* we do? The same as last year? The prez had already objected to that idea, saying she didn't want to repeat the same thing twice in a row.

Come to think of it, other clubs were doing maid cafés anyway. Well, if we did one, ours would definitely be the best. The girls in our club were simply of the highest level.

Nonetheless, the prez didn't want any kind of copy, so that was right out.

Rias went around asking all of the club members, but no one had any fresh ideas.

No one had mentioned anything even remotely related to occult research.

Rather, the main topics had revolved around our Two Great Ladies; our adorable petite cat-girl, Koneko; our beautiful second-year Church Maiden Trio comprising Asia, Xenovia, and Irina; Gasper, who was particularly popular among a certain subset of guys; and the academy's pretty boy idol, Kiba.

Lastly, there was me, the perverted sex fiend infamous throughout the school. Excluding myself, everyone had popularity on their side... It made me want to break down into tears.

Wait a minute...

Setting Kiba and me aside, everyone else here was popular with guys. Even Gasper was widely regarded as basically a girl. I had heard that he hung around with girls all the time during and between classes.

Apparently, they were worried that something might happen to Gasper if he was suddenly thrown into a group of guys, so they had decided to protect him.

"...What about an Occult Research Club popularity contest? We could find out which of our girls people like most?" I muttered thoughtlessly.

At this, the female club members all exchanged glances.

"I do wonder which of our Two Great Ladies is more beloved...," Gasper added quietly.

Rias and Akeno stared each other down. "Me, of course!" they both cried out.

They were both smiling but had intimidating auras about them.

"Oh? Did you say something, President?"

"That's my line, Akeno. Did you just say something that I can't afford to let slide?"

I was glad to see that Akeno was mostly back to her regular self, and yet... She was terrifying!

Our Two Great Ladies were moments from launching into a battle!

And so, with the two of them beginning to quarrel, our meeting came to a close. We would have to finish these discussions at a later date.

Would we really be able to decide what to do for the Academy Festival before our trip?

Azazel, as our supervising teacher, had been drinking tea in the corner of the clubroom this whole time. He had decided to supervise our activities for once, but he had spent the whole time staring out at the setting sun. "...It's already dusk," he mumbled.

At this, our faces all turned stern... Right, in that case, it was almost time for our fight with Loki.

The school bell rang out, signaling the end to all club activities for the day.

"It's still too early for Ragnarok... All right, everyone—let's go all out!"

"*Okay!*" we shouted in unison.

The sun had set, and the hour of our confrontation had arrived.

We were waiting on the rooftop of the high-rise luxury hotel where Odin was having his conference with the Japanese gods.

Likely because we were so high up, the wind was intense, buffeting all around us.

The Sitri Familia was lying in wait, positioned across the rooftop. I could make out a small figure standing in the distance.

Saji had said he would be a little late… Just what kind of special training was he being subjected to?

Saji, whatever happens, please don't wait until after *the battle to show up.*

Azazel was helping mediate the conference, so he was inside with Odin.

In his place, Baraqiel was waiting on standby with us up on the roof. Rossweisse had joined us, too, ready for combat in her full battle armor.

Tannin was even soaring up above in the sky! Under normal circumstances, a stray passerby might have seen him and caused a commotion, so he was using some kind of magic to conceal his presence from regular humans.

Vali and the others were also stationed nearby.

"It's time," the prez murmured, glancing at her watch.

The epoch-making discussions had begun inside the hotel.

Now all that was left was to wait for that no-good Loki to show his face.

What would we do if he didn't come as promised…? For all we knew, he could have disguised himself to get close to Odin. Heck, he could already be inside the hotel…

"No cheap tricks. I'm impressed." Vali's lips curled in a grin.

Had something just happened? Before I had the chance to wonder further…

Cr-crackle!

…The sky above us began to warp, and a giant hole opened in midair.

Loki descended before us with his huge ashen wolf, Fenrir!

They wasted no time launching into a head-on assault.

"Targets confirmed. Operation underway," Baraqiel stated into his communications earpiece as a gigantic barrier-type magic circle expanded around the hotel.

The chairwoman and the other members of the Sitri Familia activated their own oversized teleportation array to transport us, Loki, and Fenrir to our chosen battlefield.

Loki had clearly sensed what was going on, but he showed no sign of resistance, merely letting out a dauntless bellow of laughter.

The light enveloped us.

…

When I opened my eyes, we were in a large, open space.

Steep rocky walls surrounded us. It certainly did look like an old quarry. There was nothing to suggest that it had been used recently.

I checked to make sure the other Familia members had arrived safely, starting with the prez and counting all the way to Irina. Baraqiel and Rossweisse were there, too.

Vali and the members of his team had been transported to a spot a short distance away.

Before me stood Loki and Fenrir. No sooner did I confirm that than I initiated the countdown for my Balance Breaker.

"Not bothering with escape?" the prez inquired, clearly sarcastic.

"There's no need to flee. You would try to stop me, anyway, so it will be easiest for me to finish you all here before returning to the hotel. It's just a matter of timing. Either way, I will ensure that Odin does not continue with his mad plans."

"That's dangerous thinking," Baraqiel spat.

"*You're* the ones thinking dangerously. An alliance among three different mythological powers… To begin with, it was your biblical three great powers joining hands that set all this awry."

"Clearly, discussion with you is meaningless." With that, Baraqiel's hands began to crackle with Holy Lightning as ten black wings unfurled from his back.

My countdown was finished, too. I used a Promotion and activated my Balance Breaker as quickly as I could!

"Welsh Dragon: Balance Breaker!"
Flash!

With brilliant crimson burst, the powers of the Red Dragon Emperor solidified into a full-body suit of armor. I could feel my energy surging.

"Vanishing Dragon: Balance Breaker!" Vali also stepped out in a suit of glimmering alabaster armor.

The two of us approached our target at the same time.

Loki looked overjoyed. "Wonderful! The Two Heavenly Dragons are teaming up to defeat me! I've never been this excited!"

Whoosh!

Vali wasted no time, launching at high speed toward Loki!

At the same moment, I activated the propulsion unit on my back!

Vali would rush him from the air while I did so from the ground!

"A joint strike by Red and White! Am I the first to ever fight you both like this?!" Loki, obviously ecstatic, deployed a wide range of defensive magic circles, enough to cover his entire body.

Or so I thought, but those magic circles swiftly transformed into a multilayered shroud of enchanted light, which he then fired at us!

It was a superefficient homing attack! Several of the beams raced toward Vali, who was still weaving through the air!

Dozens more were heading toward me, too!

Vali spun through the sky like an acrobat, evading every incoming shot. I decided to push through, paying no heed to whether any of them reached me.

Thud! Thump!

Several of Loki's rays struck my body—but I could endure that much! I sped forward, closing the distance to that wicked god!

I concentrated my strength into my right fist, rushing in just above the ground at maximum acceleration toward Loki! My recently acquired dragon wings unfurled from my back.

"Boost! Boost! Boost! Boost! Boost! Boost! Boost! Boost! Boost! Boost!"
Crash!

The magic circles surrounding Loki crumbled with an audible *smash*! With our opponent's shield out of the way, Vali emitted an insane mass of demonic energy as he prepared his attack.

Something that was clearly not a regular ability began to gather in his hand.

Is that one of the Norse techniques he recently picked up?

"Here's my opening move."

Booooooooooom!

He was strafing the area! I would have to fall back at once! Talk about dangerous! That bastard Vali hadn't waited so much as a second after I had broken through Loki's defenses before striking!

His single attack engulfed a full third of the abandoned quarry!

It was absolutely insane!

When it finally came to a stop, there was only a deep crater where Loki had once stood.

Vali must have limited the range of his power, but even so, that destructive force was mind-boggling.

Once again, I was forced to realize just how abnormal my rival was.

"Bwa-ha-ha!

Laughter from up overhead!

Hurriedly looking skyward, I spotted Loki floating in midair. His robe was tattered in a few places, but apart from that, he looked unscathed.

How could he be unharmed after an attack like that? Gods really were formidable.

That meant it was time for my secret weapon! I reached for the hammer strapped to my waist—the replica Mjölnir—pouring my demonic energy into it so that it grew to optimal size!

I lifted it up over my head and swung it down at Loki.

It must have caught his attention, because I saw his eye twitch. "...Mjölnir? No, a replica? Copy or no, you're wielding a dangerous weapon there. Odin, just how far are you willing to go to ensure your meeting is a success...?!"

Judging from his reaction, Loki was more upset at Odin for letting me wield this weapon than at me for bringing it down on him.

In any other situation, the hammer would have been too heavy for me to lift, but in my Balance Breaker state, I was able to manage.

As I swung, I activated the propulsion unit on my back and braced myself!

Whoosh!

I shot toward Loki at a blinding pace.

Come on! I need it now! Lightning strong enough to fell a god! With that prayer, I let loose!

Kra-boooooooooom!

Loki moved out of the way! The impact gouged a huge hole into the ground…but the expected lightning was nowhere to be seen!

What had gone wrong? Wasn't this hammer supposed to release electricity strong enough to fry a deity?

I tried it again and again…but each time was the same as the first! Nothing at all!

I-is it defective?!

"Bwa-ha-ha!" Loki scoffed at the miserable sight. "How unfortunate. That hammer can only be used by one graced with strength and purity of heart. *Your* heart is surely wicked. That is why it won't respond to you. They say that to those who can wield Mjölnir, it is supposed to be as light as a feather. I'm guessing that for you, it's far from weightless, no?"

Seriously?! A wicked heart…? Y-yeah. I guess I can see what he means!

If you haven't noticed yet, I had a lecherous mind! Simply put, the Breast Dragon couldn't use this weapon!

"Time for me to get serious!" Loki raised a finger—and with that gesture, Fenrir, who had been waiting obediently all this time, stepped forward. "Behold Fenrir, whose fangs can rend the flesh of gods! A single bite will be enough to utterly destroy you! Do you think your-selves capable of defeating him? Give it your best effort, then!" Loki motioned once more to Fenrir.

However, that was the moment the prez raised a hand.

"Meow!"

Vrrrrr-rrrrr-rrrrr!

Kuroka laughed as magical arrays began to take shape around her, and a huge, thick chain rose up from the ground! It was Gleipnir! We were fortunate to have received it earlier than anticipated, because it was all but impossible to carry. Kuroka had hidden it away in her own private domain.

Tannin and Baraqiel seized Gleipnir from either end, with the other club members and Vali's team taking place behind. Together, they hurled the chain at Fenrir!

"Bwa-ha-ha! How futile! I took precautions against the Gleipnir long ago!"

Heedless of Loki's confident laughter, the enchanted chain, its magic boosted by dark elf magic, wrapped around Fenrir as though possessed of a mind of its own!

"Owooooooooooo...!"

The giant wolf let out an ear-rending howl that echoed through the abandoned quarry.

"Fenrir captured," Baraqiel stated curtly into his earpiece as he confirmed that the target had indeed been rendered immobile.

Yes! We had stopped Fenrir! Way to go, everyone!

It had gone exactly to plan! Those dark elves had done one heck of a job!

With Fenrir held down, the others should have been more than capable of defeating him.

Thus, all that remained was for me to deal with Loki.

I would have expected the evil god to be on the verge of losing his patience now that we had taken care of his pet...but a pleased expression was pasted on his face.

Was he still confident of victory? I watched cautiously as he raised his arms into the air.

"They might not be as high-spec, but even so—"

Vrrrrr-rrrrr.

The air on either side of him began to distort.

Wh-what now? Just what is he—?

"*Grrrrr...*"

Something began to emerge through the airborne distortion. Ashen-colored fur. Razor-sharp claws. Cold, emotionless eyes. And two huge, gaping maws!

"Sköll! Hati!"

The creatures tilted their heads to the heavens in response to Loki's voice.

"*Owoooooooooo!*"

"*Owoooooooooo!*"

The clouds shrouding the night sky were blown away, revealing a full moon.

Beneath its pale glow stood two more wolves.

More Fenrirs?! It can't be! How?! Isn't there only supposed to be one?!

I wasn't the only one astonished by this development. Shock was written large on everyone else's faces, too. Excepting Vali, of course. He looked rather pleased.

With the two additional Fenrirs waiting on his command, Loki called out, "I transformed a troll woman of the Ironwood into a wolf and had her breed with Fenrir. The result was these two. They aren't quite as formidable as their father, but their fangs are extremely potent nonetheless. I'm sure they're easily enough to slay a god, let alone you."

So Fenrir had children...? How was I supposed to have known that?! Midgardsormr hadn't mentioned it! Maybe he wasn't aware?! This was bad!

Loki turned to the two new Fenrirs. "Go, Sköll and Hati! Rend those who dared to capture your father!"

Whoosh!

The two wolves raced forward like wind! One of them charged at my friends, while the other made for Team Vali!

We didn't have any more chains! We had used our only one to subdue Fenrir!

"Hmph! A mere lowly dog!"

Booooooooooom!

Tannin let loose with his fire breath! As expected of a Dragon King, those roiling flames quickly enveloped the junior Fenrir!

However, the wolf continued forward. He had certainly taken damage, but he hadn't flinched in the slightest!

We would have to defeat them both head-on! As I glanced toward my allies, Loki began to unleash a fresh wave of overpowered magic attacks!

Swoosh!

I managed to dodge the oncoming assault by a hair's breadth, but one shot still carved cleanly through a part of my armor! Uh-oh! A direct hit would spell disaster! Standing up to a god was never going to be easy, but cutting into my Boosted Gear Scale Mail was just unfair!

"...I won't be able to use my halving powers properly against a divine being. We'll have to wear him down a fraction at a time!" Vali shouted.

Boom! Boom! Booooooooooom!

He loosed a volley of Norse magic techniques from both hands. Loki tried to deflect them with his own powers but proved unable to stop them all. Unfortunately, those few that did connect with him didn't seem to bother him much.

"I commend you, White Dragon Emperor! You've taught yourself Norse magic! And in so little time, no less! Regrettably..."

Loki hurled another massive wave of power that scintillated in all the colors of the rainbow. Vali readied himself to meet it, expanding the wings of light stretching out from his back.

"*Divide! Divide! Divide! Divide! Divide!*"

Having activated his Divine Dividing, he continued to reduce the potency of Loki's attack.

"I can still halve the strength of an attack without coming into direct contact with it. But it *is* taking a lot out of me."

Was that a ranged halving technique? One that, even if not effective against Loki himself, could still be used against his attacks? Evidently, Vali was developing new abilities of his own. Terrifying!

Nonetheless, some of those attacks managed to break through, striking Vali's armor! Pieces of the suit cracked and shattered, but Vali hurriedly restored them.

"Gooooooooooo!"

"Boost! Boost! Boost! Boost! Boost! Boost! Boost! Boost! Boost!"

With no time to waste, I unleashed a humongous Dragon Shot aimed squarely at Loki! If the hammer was no good, maybe an attack like this would do something!

Boooooooooom!

Loki met it head-on, his bold expression unflinching.

Boom!

Then he sent my attack racing toward Vali! It sped toward him rapidly, but fortunately, he evaded.

"Bwa-ha-ha! The White Dragon Emperor boasts well-honed strength, while the Red Dragon Emperor attacks with tremendous energy. Though devoid of technique or skill, you aren't to be underestimated, I see! Hmm… Impressive! An attack filled with raw spirit! Oh, how it resonates within me! Just how much of your will did you pour into that last one?"

Deflecting my attack had seemingly taken more out of Loki than his tone suggested, because his hands were spasming a bit.

Were we truly outmatched here? No way could I have done it alone, but with Vali, I still had a chance! So long as I still had some energy left, I could transfer it to him or even to any of my other allies…

Then I recalled the warning I had received—that if I were to focus on support, Loki would concentrate his attention on my friends instead.

"You, White Dragon Emperor, are quick on your feet! Thus, I believe I'll focus instead on the Red Dragon Emperor! It would be a nuisance if you were to transfer that immense power of yours to someone else! Crushing you first seems best!"

Damn! He knew what I was thinking!

Loki pointed his arm at me to indicate I was his first target.

"How dare you ignore me!"

Swoosh!

Vali rocketed in, positioning himself behind Loki as he readied an attack!

Go for it!

Vali had gathered a titanic mass of demonic power into his hands! Not even Loki should have been capable of stopping it.

Crunch!

One of the Fenrirs caught Vali in his maw.

"Ghk!"

Blood shot from Vali's mouth! Those fangs carved through his silver armor with ease, digging straight into his flesh.

The junior Fenrir's jaws grew stained with crimson.

Wait... That isn't a junior Fenrir, it's the parent...! What's he doing here?! How'd he free himself from the chain?!

I frantically looked around and saw that the two junior Fenrirs were holding Gleipnir between their teeth! They had only been pretending to fight the others—their real goal had been to release their father!

"Bwa-ha-ha! It looks like I've crushed the *White* Dragon Emperor first after all!"

"Vali!"

I restored the replica Mjölnir to its original size before rushing after Fenrir to free Vali from his jaw! This hadn't gone at all as planned!

Vali! If you drop out here, the plan will be up in smoke! Sorry about this, but we need your strength right now!

Fenrir regarded me casually, merely turning to meet me head-on. He wasn't scared of me at all!

"You damn mongrel!"

I lashed out with a punch to his nose!

Slash!

At the same time, Fenrir cleaved through the air with a clawed paw! It tore through my Scale Mail with ease...!

Arghhhhh!

Blood splattered from my mouth and stomach. This was bad. If Vali died here and I was knocked out of the fight, too…

"Ngh! I won't let you take them!"

Tannin swooped down to back us up, breathing a massive ball of fire. The heat was incredible! Fenrir didn't give any ground, however.

It was a showdown between two real-life monsters. They were almost identical in size, but the dragon clearly appeared to be the stronger of the two.

"Owoooooooooo!"

A piercing cry sounded, pushing Tannin's flames aside and shaking the whole battlefield! I couldn't believe it! That wolf could seriously dispel an attack from a Dragon King so easily?!

Swoosh!

In a flash, Fenrir vanished from view!

Crunch!

I could hear the sound of something being torn.

"Gwaughhhhh!" Tannin screamed in agony.

The old dragon was getting rent apart! His blood stained the ground!

That wolf had moved at incredible speed, slashing the Dragon King with his claws!

What was I supposed to do?! A legendary dragon, my mighty and imposing mentor, was being mercilessly attacked!

My stomach contorted in frustration. I thought dragons were supposed to be the strongest of beings! Prouder and more formidable than anything else! Yet that ashen-gray wolf had brought that belief crashing down!

Still coughing up blood, Tannin broke open something in his mouth near his back teeth, then swallowed it. With a burst of smoke, his wounds vanished. He had just used a vial of Phoenix Tears. We had been provided with some in preparation for this battle.

I, too, pulled a vial from my waist, sprinkling it on my wounds.

Fshhhhh…

Steam rose up from my skin as the tears mended my injuries.

...That was close.

Fenrir's claws had dug deep into my flesh. Talk about tremendous attack power! My Red Dragon Emperor Scale Mail was nothing compared to that! No wonder that creature had crushed Vali's armor and shredded Tannin's body without trouble. Everything about Fenrir—his fangs, his claws, his every attack—was off the charts. How could that creature possibly overcome three legendary dragons so effortlessly...?!

That wolf was totally unfair!

Vali and I, the vanguard of our force, had each received several vials of Phoenix Tears. Unfortunately, as Fenrir was still gripping Vali in his mouth, it would be useless to use any on him. First, I would have to get the wolf to release him.

There was no winning a head-on fight with Fenrir. The wolf had to be at least as strong as Ddraig in his original form. I couldn't draw on Ddraig's full power, though, so any fight would be risky.

What about my Juggernaut Drive? I thought.

That might work, but I would definitely end up dying... Still, if worst came to worst, I might have to do just that. I would have to be ready. It was certainly preferable to letting the prez, Asia, and all the others get killed.

At this rate, we would just end up exhausting our supply of Phoenix Tears, and we still needed to save Vali!

"Perhaps I'll have you face these creatures as well?" Loki mused.

A shadow expanded beneath his feet—and multiple giant snakes emerged.

Worst of all, I recognized their forms. Sure, they were considerably smaller in size, but there was no mistaking them!

"Mass-produced Midgardsormr clones?!" Tannin spat in disgust.

He was right! They were the spitting image of the Dragon King Midgardsormr. Although they were no bigger than Tannin, Loki had called up five of them!

"Roooooaaaaar!"

The mass-produced dragons began to breathe columns of fire!

"Not if I can help it!"

Boooooooooom!

Tannin brushed those flames aside with his own scorching breath.

Real-life dragons packed an incredible punch!

Still, this situation was quickly going from bad to worse! My allies weren't ready to call it quits just yet, though!

"Damn you!"

"We'll be done for if we stick to defense! Everyone, attack!"

That was Bikou, followed by the prez. Both Team Vali and the Gremory Familia were engulfed in a bitter battle to the death with the two junior Fenrirs.

"Holy Lightning!"

Cr-craaaaash!

Baraqiel unleashed an electric volley at least ten times stronger than anything I had ever seen Akeno use. But even so...

The two Fenrir spawn lashed out again, completely unfazed. They must have sustained considerable damage by now...but their battle fervor looked to override everything else!

"All my training with the Red Dragon Emperor wasn't just for show!" Kiba cried out, dashing around the field at breakneck speed as he followed the junior Fenrirs' movements before bringing down a Holy Demon Sword on one of them. His blade stabbed through the creature's head, sending blood flying.

Whoa! Way to go, Kiba!

"Gwaugh!"

Xenovia, who had tried to land a strike of her own, was thrown backward by the junior Fenrir's counterattack! Blood spewed from her wound!

"Xenovia!" Irina cried out, using one of the vials of Phoenix Tears on her. No sooner had she done so than she summoned up a spear of light. That kind of weapon wouldn't deal fatal damage, but it was enough to buy a brief respite.

The Phoenix Tears instantly mended Xenovia's wounds, and she stood with Durendal and Ascalon ready.

"Gasper! Blind him! Take away his vision! Koneko, take advantage of that chance to use your sage magic on him. Target anywhere you can!" the prez instructed.

With that, Gasper's body transformed into a swarm of clicking bats, quickly gathering around the child-Fenrir's face and obscuring his vision.

Nice move, Gasper!

"I'll disrupt his *qi*, even if only a little!" Koneko said, using that window to ensure her punch found purchase.

It was only a single strike to the leg, but it appeared to be enough. A blow imbued with sage magic could pass all the way through the body, disrupting its target's life force. It didn't have to be a critical hit, just enough to give everyone else the time they needed.

"Xenovia, now!"

With the prez's next instruction, Xenovia braced herself with her twin blades. "I'm still raring to go!" she cried, voice echoing.

Booooooooooom!

Just as she had done against Diodora's Familia, Xenovia poured her aura into a huge wave of energy, sending it racing toward the Fenrir spawn!

Craaaaash!

The junior Fenrir was completely enveloped by that attack... By the time the wave passed, it had inflicted two deep wounds, but still, the creature had yet to fall! Even that wasn't enough!

"Try this!"

Cl-cl-clang!

Kiba summoned a trap of Holy Demon Swords around the child-Fenrir's feet, temporarily pinning him in place! Next, he flew toward him like a streak of lightning, cleaving through the monster's body!

Crackle! Cr-crash!

Akeno followed suit, bringing down a hail of lightning!

Our Familia was stronger than that junior Fenrir!

"How about this?"

"*Roooooaaaaar!*"

Tannin let fly a high-powered burst of flame right into one of the Midgardsormr copies a short distance away! A burning sea surged from his maw and flooded the quarry!

The serpent-dragon writhed in pain amid the flames! That was to be expected from the fire of a former Dragon King! Before long, the Midgardsormr copy had been reduced to ash.

"Again!"

"*Roooooaaaaar!*"

Tannin took a deep breath before releasing an oversized ball of flame from his mouth toward another of the mass-produced dragons! The blast was so powerful that it blew a huge crater into the ground!

Incredible! Those Dragon King copies stood no chance against the real thing. Tannin was amazing! But Fenrir was impossibly strong, too!

"No you don't!" Rossweisse activated a Nordic spell circle to back up Tannin!

Magic bullets rained down from above, tearing through the amassed enemies.

That strike certainly looked to have dealt considerable damage to the Midgardsormr copies. That Valkyrie was impressive!

"Recovery! And for you as well!"

Asia was sending out her healing aura to all of us who got hurt. Her powers helped us keep fighting long after we would otherwise have been done for. However, she was healing one person after another without end. It was clear from her expression that she was growing weary. On top of that, she knew that any one of us could die if not for her healing ability, undoubtedly adding immense psychological pressure.

Nonetheless, we needed her Sacred Gear to keep going. The Phoenix Tears we had brought with us wouldn't be enough to restore all the injuries we were sustaining.

You can do it, Asia! If you find yourself in danger, I'll be there to help you!

Team Vali was focusing on the other child-Fenrir and looked to be having a similar degree of success.

"Hey, hey, hey, hey, hey!"

Bikou lashed out with his Nyoibou, striking the creature again and again!

"Extend!"

Thud!

Bikou's staff stretched to a ridiculous length, slamming hard against the child-Fenrir's head!

"Ha-ha-ha! Slow down a little!"

Next, Kuroka used some sort of technique to turn the ground at the creature's feet into mud.

Unable to move, the junior Fenrir found himself at the mercy of Arthur's Holy King Sword!

"Perhaps I'll take one of your eyes first?"

Slash!

The Holy King Sword gouged the creature's left eye right out of its socket!

"Next, your claws."

He went on to carve through the creature's front paw! Trust me when I say that it was a terribly cruel attack! And it was made all the more horrifying when he did it with such a dispassionate face!

"And now for those dangerous fangs! Collbrande is more than capable of obliterating a measly spawn of Fenrir!"

Slash!

The Holy King Sword passed through the air, slicing away the monster's teeth!

"*Gyaaaaahhhhhhh!*"

As was to be expected, the child-Fenrir let out an agonized shriek at the loss of his eye, claws, and fangs.

So those three are Vali's allies... They're strong. Even if their opponent was a child compared to the adult Fenrir, the way they dispatched him so handily was abnormal.

And the three of them didn't even appear to be exerting themselves.

More impressive still, they were continuing to carry out their designated objectives even when their leader, Vali, was in dire trouble. Our Familia would never have been able to do that.

"…Issei Hyoudou."

That was Vali! Though still trapped between Fenrir's fangs, he was calling out to me! It was painful just to look at him!

"…I'll leave Loki and the rest to you, Bikou, and the others."

He can't mean…, I thought in disbelief.

"I will destroy this parent Fenrir," he added.

At that, Loki broke into laughter. "Bwa-ha-ha! How, exactly? White Dragon Emperor, you are already all but dead! Do you intend to degrade your name more than you already have?"

"Don't you dare mock Vali Lucifer, one of the Two Heavenly Dragons…"

Whoa…

Vali glared at Loki with such cold intensity that *I* felt unnerved.

The next moment, he started muttering something under his breath, and a divine aura began to slowly bleed from his armor in every color of the rainbow.

"Gwaaaaauuuuugh!"

"*I have awakened…*"

"*Destroy them!*"

"*Destroy them all!*"

Voices that didn't belong to Vali echoed throughout the quarry… These must have been the lingering resentments of the previous White Dragon Emperors who had laid dormant within his Sacred Gear. I couldn't believe this was what those curses sounded like! It was only now, when I saw them for myself, did I fully realize that I had been trying to talk entities of pure darkness into seeing reason!

"*My quest for domination stole everything away from me and rendered me thus, a Heavenly Dragon…*"

"The dream is over!"

"The illusion has begun!"

"I envy the infinite, dwell on the illusion..."

"Everything!"

"Give me everything!"

"I am the White Dragon Dynast—"

""""""""""""""And I shall lead you into sterile infinity!""""""""""""""""

"Juggernaut Drive!"

An intense light filled the entire abandoned quarry, spilling from Fenrir's mouth and swallowing the wolf himself.

Whoaaaaa!

The power was so intense that I couldn't properly measure it all. My senses were practically paralyzed! This was—

"Kuroka! Teleport Fenrir and me to the place!" exclaimed Vali, still glowing brilliantly.

In response, Kuroka flashed Vali a broad grin, arching her hand toward him and twisting her fingers through the air.

When I looked carefully, I saw that Vali's armor was gradually transforming.

Is this due to his Juggernaut Drive? So that was what happened to me...

Suddenly, I realized the enchanted chain that was supposed to have captured Fenrir had been transported to Vali, too! That must have been Kuroka's doing. In his current state, Vali had a good chance of succeeding with Gleipnir!

Vrrrrrrrrrr!

Countless layers of magic energy wrapped around Vali and Fenrir, who were encased in a giant mass of light.

Before long, the two of them had melted into the night scenery, completely vanishing!

"Vali!" I shouted, but there was no response...

It was my first time ever witnessing a Juggernaut Drive for myself, but there was no mistaking it. That bastard Vali had initiated it for himself!

Was he hoping to take Fenrir somewhere far from the battlefield by brute force? And what was that "place" he had mentioned...? Had I been right all along? Was he really up to something else entirely?

No, that couldn't be it. Vali probably wanted to settle this somewhere removed from the rest of us. Perhaps he'd schemed as much beforehand.

According to Azazel, Vali was capable of using his Juggernaut Drive for short periods of time by feeding his demonic energy into his Sacred Gear in place of his life force. Even so, he still couldn't wield it freely... It would probably take very little to make him go berserk. The Juggernaut Drive could very well consume him just like it had me.

An abrupt scream brought me back to the battle around me.

"Akeno!"

It was the prez! I spun around and saw Akeno about to be mauled by a junior Fenrir!

Don't you even dare!

No way was I going to let that monster hurt her! My beloved great lady! My dearest Akeno!

I glanced at Loki and set the propulsion unit on my back to maximum! Both of my dragon wings had already fully expanded.

"Jet!"

The voice of the jewels embedded in my armor rang out as I approached my target. Swift as I was, I still wasn't going to make it, but I had to!

"You're riddled with openings!" Loki fired off another magical attack my way.

Boooooooooom!

Thankfully, a huge fireball and a burst of light had caught the projectile before it struck me!

"I don't think so!"

"That's right!"

It was Tannin and Rossweisse! After offering them a word of mental gratitude, I scanned the area and realized only one Midgardsormr copy remained.

Tannin and Rossweisse still appeared raring to go! The two of them had practically annihilated those replica Dragon Kings!

This wasn't the time to be focusing on them, however, because the worst thing I could possibly imagine was about to play out directly in front of me.

The child-Fenrir's fangs bore down on Akeno!

Slash!

There came a dull sound of fangs rending meat! However, the one who caught the blow wasn't Akeno, but Baraqiel!

The fallen angel had thrown himself in harm's way to protect his daughter, and the child-Fenrir's fangs had torn clean through his back.

"Gah!"

Blood poured from the man's mouth and wounds.

Stunned, Akeno asked, "…Why?"

"…Because I don't want to lose you, too," Baraqiel managed weakly.

Akeno's expression told me she didn't know what to make of all this.

"Hey!"

Thump!

I slammed my fist into the child-Fenrir from the side, forcing him to release the fallen angel and jump backward.

"Asia!" I called out.

Within a split second, the former nun sent pale-green light toward Baraqiel! As that glow washed over him, his wounds slowly healed.

It was enough to stanch the bleeding, but he was still in no shape to keep fighting. Baraqiel had probably lost just as much energy as he had blood, and he had been drained of a *lot* of the latter.

Visibly upset, Akeno could only stammer out, "I—I…"

"…Calm down, Akeno. The battle isn't over yet!" Baraqiel instructed, voice still frail.

Akeno. Please don't cry. It's okay. I'll protect you.

There was something I had to know. Did she really hate her father? I had to make sure.

I subtly activated Boob-Lingual and asked Akeno's breasts to shed light on that deep-held secret.

Hey, Akeno's breasts. Can you hear me? Does Akeno truly resent Baraqiel?

"..."

Her boobs didn't give an answer. Had my technique failed? Or was Akeno so shocked that even her breasts had been left speechless?

But then a soft voice spoke up.

"I'm not Akeno Himejima's breasts. I'm a breast sprite."

...

...Huh?

"...Who are you?!" I shouted, startled and pointing to Akeno's chest.

Akeno and Baraqiel were even more shocked by my abrupt outburst!

"Please stay calm. I'm speaking to you through this girl's breasts."

This was getting stranger by the second!

H-huuuuuuuuuuh?! What?! What is this?!

Flabbergasted, I demanded, "No! Wh-who are you?! Answer me!"

"I am a sprite in the service of the god of breasts. Your unquenchable thirst for breasts summoned me here."

No way! My Boob-Lingual technique had reached an altogether different recipient! Was such a thing possible?!

"T-Tannin!"

The former Dragon King was embroiled in battle with Loki! But this was a question that required his wisdom!

"What's going on?! Did something happen?! More breasts?!" he cried back impatiently in response to my panicked voice.

"Which religion does the god of breasts come from?!"

The old dragon seemed unable to muster a reply to my inquiry.

For some reason, when I glanced around, my allies and opponents alike had all paused what they were doing, staring my way incredulously. A second passed, and Tannin called out to the prez: "Lady Rias! You need to heal that dimwit's head! He's suffered a critical blow!"

No! I'm fine, you old geezer! There's nothing wrong with me!

"Issei! Hang in there! It's just a hallucination! You're hearing things! Ah, how could this have happened?! Fenrir's poison is affecting his mind!"

The prez had the wrong idea, too! She seemed to think my brain was malfunctioning! But Fenrir's fangs hadn't even scratched me!

A warm glow wrapped around my head.

Thank you, Asia, but I'm fine. This doesn't require your attention.

"You've got the wrong idea! Akeno's breasts just said they're some breast sprite!"

As I tried to explain, Baraqiel shouted me down, clearly furious. "You...! You would accuse my daughter of something so incomprehensibly obscene...?! You accursed Breast Dragon...!"

He was totally incensed! Fierce waves of Holy Lightning were literally coursing down his body!

Asia's healing aura wrapped around my head once more.

Thanks again, Asia. But really, I'm fine!

"N-no, listen, everyone," Ddraig spoke up. *"I can hear the voice of this breast sprite, too... From what I can sense, it hails from an unknown plane of existence. I'm sorry it's come to this, but my host looks to have attracted the messenger of a god from another world."*

Yes! Thanks, partner! I knew I could rely on you!

"That's insane!"

"Impossible!"

"Ddraig has gone crazy, too!"

No! Now they weren't willing to believe a dragon, either!

"Bwaaaaaugh! No one trusts me! All because of you, Breast Dragon! I haven't done anything wrong! Partner! Partneeeeer!"

Ddraig was in tears! It felt like I had been making him cry a lot lately... I needed to apologize at some point.

Ah!

This time, I could feel Asia's healing aura coursing through the jewels across my armor!

Asia! I'm fully healed here! My HP is at its max! Do I still look like I need more?!

"Hey, Switch Princess! Go and let him hit your knockers! He needs 'em now!" Bikou said to the prez.

"...R-right, maybe I should..."

I had been sure the prez would come out with some sort of complaint in response to that, but had Bikou truly convinced her?!

"Listen carefully, Breast Dragon Emperor," Akeno's breasts called to me.

A-and they had just addressed me as the Breast Dragon Emperor! Dammit! Where had they learned that name?!

"You must give your ear to the thoughts of this shrine maiden and summon the powers of the god of breasts."

What now? I didn't quite follow, but whatever that was supposed to mean, it did sound impressive.

"The god of breasts is merciful and grants divine protection to those who seek boobs."

...Nope, none of this was adding up! I *did* wish to hear Akeno's honest feelings, however.

I-in that case, sprite, can you share her feelings only with me, Baraqiel, and Akeno herself?

"Very well... Listen carefully to her innermost feelings."

When I closed my eyes, a scene appeared in the back of my mind.

I could hear the voice of a young girl singing.

"Where do you live, friend? Where are you? Where in Higo, where are you?"

She was in the courtyard of a single-story house, bouncing a ball as she sang a nursery rhyme to herself.

"Akeno? Are you there?"

A woman who looked identical to Akeno called out to the young girl.

"Mama!" Akeno said happily upon seeing her mother, running over to embrace her.

The woman had silky black hair and looked like a particularly warm and kind individual. She had a beautiful look about her, but also one that seemed somehow fleeting.

"Mama. Will Papa be coming home today?"

"Dear me, Akeno. Are you planning on going somewhere together?"

Akeno flashed her mother a joyous smile at this question. *"If he comes home soon, we're going to take the bus and go shopping!"*

"I was so lonely."

That... That was Akeno's voice, I realized.

The scene had changed. Now Baraqiel was helping the young Akeno take a bath.

"I don't hate your wings, Papa. They're black, but they're so soft and pretty, just like my hair!"

"Is that right? Thank you, Akeno."

"All I wanted was for him to always be there with us."

Akeno's mother was braiding her daughter's hair on the veranda outside the house.

"Hey, Mama. Does Papa really like me?"

"Of course he does." The woman smiled as she gently tied back her daughter's locks.

"I wasn't able to see him as often as I wanted."

The vision underwent another shift.

Now the room was in tatters. Furniture had been knocked carelessly to the floor, and the tatami mats had gruesome tears in them. The

table had been upended, scattering the remains of the evening meal across the floor.

It was a complete mess.

"Hand over the child, that spawn of a wicked, blackhearted fallen angel."

A group of what looked like shamanist practitioners had surrounded Akeno and her mother.

"You can't have her! She's my daughter! She's too important and precious! And he loves her, too! I won't let you take her!" Akeno's mother shouted, shielding her child.

"...You've allowed a fallen angel to defile you. You leave us no choice."

One of the shamans pulled out a katana and brought it down—

"Mamaaaaa!"

The next vision was of Baraqiel stained in crimson.

The blood belonged to the shamans. He had killed them all.

"Mama! Nooooo! Mamaaaaa!"

A sobbing and distraught Akeno was trying to rouse her fallen mother...

"...Shuri..." Baraqiel reached out to his wife, his hands trembling.

"Don't touch her!" Akeno shrieked, batting her father's hand away.

"Why?! Why didn't you stay here with us?! We were always waiting for you, Papa! Always! You said you were coming home early today! You said you were taking the day off! If you were here, Mama wouldn't have died!"

"..."

"I heard what they said! That you're a blackhearted fallen angel, and evil! They said you fallen angels are bad people! And that I'm bad, too, because I have black wings as well! If you and I didn't have these black wings, Mama wouldn't be dead! I hate them! I hate everything! You! These wings! Everyone! I hate them all!"

"I knew it wasn't my father's fault. But... If I didn't try to tell myself that it was, I wouldn't be able to keep on going... Because I'm...weak... And lonely... All I wanted was for us to live together, the three of us..."

*   *   *

I could hear the voice of Akeno's mother within my head.

"Akeno."

It was an unmistakably kind and gentle voice.

"Whatever happens, you must believe in your father. It's true that he may have hurt a great many people in the past. And yet..."

Perhaps it was an illusion. Nonetheless, I could see her clearly.

Akeno's mother was gently embracing her daughter and Baraqiel.

"And yet he most definitely loves you and me. So, Akeno, please make sure you love him back."

When I regained consciousness, Akeno was sitting beside me—bawling her eyes out.

"Mother...! I...! I wanted to see Father more! I wanted him to pat me on the head! I wanted to go play with him! Father... Mother... I wanted us all to live together, the three of us, to spend more time together...!"

These were Akeno's true feelings, which had remained hidden to her until now.

It looked like the visions I'd glimpsed had also played out for Akeno and Baraqiel.

Baraqiel was lying on his side after having heard Akeno's confession. "Not a day went by...when I didn't think about Shuri...and you...," he assured softly, reaching out to Akeno with a trembling hand.

Akeno took that hand in her own. "...Father."

That was when it happened.

Flaaaaash!

Every jewel embedded into my Red Dragon Emperor Scale Mail burst with light—as did the Mjölnir replica.

...Whatever it was, it was incredibly powerful...

"Breast Dragon Emperor? Can you hear me, Breast Dragon Emperor?"

It was the voice of the breast sprite, speaking to me through Akeno's chest.

"You have saved this girl's feelings, and her breasts, too. As thanks, the god of breasts grants you divine protection—"

Boooooooooom!
A massive quantity of energy erupted from every part of my armor.
"*Be careful, Breast Dragon Emperor. The power of the god of breasts can be used only once.*"
Whatever was going on, if this sprite and its god were granting me a special power-up, I would happily take it!
The power surging within the Mjölnir replica was beyond anything I had ever sensed before. It was far greater than Vali's powers or mine!
"I sense an unfamiliar god-class power. A...god of breasts...? From another world? This Red Dragon Emperor incarnation is full of surprises!" Loki said as he removed his cloak, enlarging his shadow!
From that shadow, another five of those mass-produced Midgardsormr copies emerged! How could there be more of them?!
This was already a seriously deadly battle! There was no end to it! Who would have thought it would be this hard to fight against a single god and his subordinates?! Was there no end to this army of junior Fenrirs and fake Dragon Kings?! Our supply of Phoenix Tears wouldn't be able to keep up, nor would Asia's healing power!
Suddenly, a dark shroud raced past me.
Booooooooooooooooooooom!
A black flame-like substance snaked across the ground, swelling and wrapping around Loki, the two child-Fenrirs, and the new Midgardsormr copies!
Wh-what is it this time?! A god of asses?!
"—! That jet-black aura?! Is that Vritra, the Prison Dragon?!"
Vritra?! Saji?! Now that I stopped to think about it, it *did* look like Saji's aura. But he'd never had any kind of fire abilities.
A huge magic circle appeared on the ground, and from its center, ebon flame in the shape of a dragon began to emerge.
"*Issei Hyoudou. Can you hear me? This is Shemhazai, the lieutenant governor of Grigori.*"
An unfamiliar voice sounded in the earpiece I was wearing for emergency communication. It was one of Azazel's colleagues.

"Ah, hi. Are you the one who sent this black dragon here?"

"*Yes. Azazel asked me to send him along once we were done with his training.*"

"So that really is Saji?!"

Whoa, so he had become a literal flame dragon. And a pitch-black one, no less...

"*Yes. It seems that Azazel made a slight miscalculation. We began his training, but he ended up in this state. We were out of time, so we decided to send him into battle as is. It does appear that he can't quite distinguish between friend and foe at the moment, however.*"

Uh, was that really okay? These fallen angels could be quite reckless at times.

"What did you do, exactly?" I questioned.

"*We gave him all of Vritra's Sacred Gears.*"

That sounded extremely negligent...

All I could do was try to compel my lips into adopting a forced smile.

"*When Vritra was subdued long ago, his soul was divided into numerous Sacred Gears,*" Shemhazai elaborated. "*Because of that, there a great many Vritra-type Sacred Gear hosts. Nonetheless, all of their Sacred Gears belong to one of four categories: Absorption Line, Blaze Black Flare, Delete Field, or Shadow Prison. These Sacred Gears were hidden in each of their hosts with some differences in specifications. Our organization, Grigori, has collected several of them, and so we installed them into Saji. His previous contact with you already roused Vritra's consciousness, so Azazel predicted that integrating the Sacred Gears together could make him fully emerge.*"

So that was why Azazel had taken him...?

"*We succeeded in combining those Sacred Gears, and indeed, in reviving Vritra's mind, too... Unfortunately, he immediately went out of control when we did so. The good news is that Saji's own consciousness appears to be intact, so if you speak to him through Ddraig, you should be able to reach him. The rest is up to you. Can you do it?*"

"...Sure, I'll try. If worst comes to worst, I'll do my best to stop him."

Saji, or rather, the black flames of Vritra, had completely enveloped Loki and his minions, keeping them locked in place. The blaze fluttered as if with a mind of its own, a coiling serpent-like shape writhing around its prey.

"Gah! What is this fire?! I can't move...! Ngh! It's draining my energy! I-is this the Black Dragon?! I've heard of an old Dragon King who specializes in manipulating flame, but could this truly be him?!" Loki was thrashing around, his expression fraught with obvious terror.

The junior Fenrirs and the Midgardsormr copies were equally unnerved, flailing wildly as they tried to escape.

"*Vritra has always been capable of more than direct attacks. He might be the weakest of all the Dragon Kings, but in terms of the diversity of his techniques, he is unmatched.*"

"...Whoa. Er, Lieutenant Governor? If there are other Vritra Sacred Gears, can we make more fighters like this?"

"*The likelihood of that is close to zero. To begin with, combining Sacred Gears is a dangerous thing to attempt. If anything were to go wrong, the recipient would all but certainly die. This was a special case. You and Saji are friends and understand each other exceptionally well. That played a part in restoring Vritra's consciousness. It would be extremely difficult to repeat that process. Just so you know, adding new powers to him hasn't changed his Evil Piece. His primary technique remains the Absorption Line. His base stats shouldn't be too affected, either.*"

So this was something that only Saji could pull off? This Vritra power of his certainly looked formidable!

"*In any event, Saji won't be able to maintain this power for long. Defeat your enemies while they're still immobilized,*" stated Shemhazai.

"Got it!"

Yeah! All right then—let's settle this!

I wrapped my hand around the Mjölnir, enlarging it to the size of a giant hammer! It was so light this time! Right, it was *supposed* to feel as light as a feather! And it did!

"Prez! Bikou! The child-Fenrirs can't move through these flames! Let's finish them off now!"

The two of them—no, everyone else, too—nodded in agreement and launched into a fresh wave of attacks against the child-Fenrirs and the Midgardsormr copies.

"I will defeat all of Odin's enemies!" Rossweisse, too, deployed a wall of magic circles around her, unleashing fresh projectile attacks in all directions!

Booooooooooom!

Those projectiles came crashing down on the immobile child-Fenrirs and Midgardsormr copies, dealing massive damage!

Because Saji was absorbing their powers, they were gradually weakening!

"Saji, can you hear me?" I asked, trying to reach out to him inside that black, fiery dragon through my Sacred Gear.

"...Ugh."

Ah! A response!

"Saji! It's me, Issei."

"H-Hyoudou...? I... What's happening to me...? I feel so hot right now I could melt..."

"You need to hold on! Assert your will! You made a really cool entrance a minute ago, so keep going until you've finished the job, and then you can go down!"

"...What should I do?"

"What can you see around yourself?"

"...I'm surrounded by black flames, and there's a huge wolf, and a bunch of dragons, too..."

"Keep them tied down. Concentrate on that. Anyway, you need to focus your thoughts! Can you see any human-sized enemies?"

"...Yeah... I don't know how to explain it, but I can sense some unknown magical power in him. And he's trying to use it to extinguish the flames..."

"That's the boss! Don't let him put your flames out! Focus your thoughts and hold him down! I'll do the rest! I'll finish this!"

I tightened my grip around the hammer.

Cr-crackle!

This time, there was lightning running through it. I wouldn't miss! It was going to pummel that jerk god!

"Jet!"

I set the propulsion unit on my back to maximum, unfurled my dragon wings, and shot straight toward Loki!

Loki, in turn, unleashed a magical attack from the palm of his hand! There could be no dodging it now! Part of me wanted to use the hammer as a shield, but if I ended up draining its power that way, this would all have been for nothing!

Vrrrrr-rrrrr-rrrrr!

I met Loki's attack head-on! It hurt! The blow dealt severe damage to my armor!

The blast even penetrated my suit and reached my body. My chest, my gut, my hips and legs, everything was filled with a severe jolt of pain.

Vrrrrr!

The last one even scored a direct hit on my helmet!

I wasn't going to have time to restore my Scale Mail or heal my injuries! I would just have to push forward!

Crash!

Loki broke free from Saji's fiery snare! Uh-oh! He may have been rotten, but he *was* definitely a deity!

"Did you think *this* would be enough to hold down the great Loki?!" he bellowed, soaring up high into the sky!

He was trying to run away!

"Stop right there!" I shouted.

Loki, however, merely laughed at me. "It's futile, Red Dragon Emperor. I will withdraw. Bwa-ha-ha! Know this: I will make a third entrance and usher in new chaos—"

Bzzzzz-zaaaaa-zzzzzz!

A huge surge of lighting and thunder burst forth, completely ensnaring Loki as he gloated.

I hurriedly turned and saw Akeno and Baraqiel with their hands outstretched. Both of them were flying with the characteristic black wings of fallen angels.

Ha. Incredible! A father-daughter joint attack, with Holy Lightning, no less!

"Wh-what?!

Loki plummeted to the ground, smoke rising up from his charred limbs! It didn't look like he had taken much damage, but at least he hadn't escaped!

Roooooaaaaarrrrr!

Saji's ebon fire wound around Loki once more! Good timing, Saji!

"Impossible! I destroyed your measly barrier!"

Loki was clearly taken aback by this, but Saji's strength of will here was on the same level as mine! He wasn't about to give up easily!

"*...Do it, Hyoudou!*"

Right! Leave it to me, Saji! I thought confidently. Then I set my sights on my target and steadied my aim before lifting the hammer aloft!

"Take this! A Hyoudou-style Mjölniiiiir!"

Wham!

I drove the head of the huge hammer down into Loki's body!

"Nooooow! Let's do this, Ddraig!" I shouted at the top of my lungs.

"*Ready!*"

"*Boost! Boost! Boost! Boost! Boost! Boost! Boost! Boost! Boost! Boost!*"

"*Transfer!*"

I sent all the power accumulated in my body into the Mjölnir replica! Immediately, an unbelievable amount of lightning and thunder erupted from the weapon!

Baaaaaaaaaaannnnnnnnnnngggggggggggg!

An overwhelmingly explosive attack collided directly with Loki.

The battered god collapsed to the ground, plumes of gray vapor streaming from him.

"...Is this why the biblical God created Balance Breakers...? These so-called Longinuses, capable of slaying the divine... Did he foresee an event like this...? Why else would he leave humans with the means to destroy their betters?"

With those final words, Loki lost consciousness.

At the same moment, the two child-Fenrirs and the Midgardsormr copies were similarly defeated.

"Excellent work, Breast Dragon Emperor. I look forward to meeting you again one day."

The voice of the breast sprite was fading away. Had it completed its task? Hold on, what had its task actually been in the first place?!

...I-it looked like I had come into contact with yet more new and unfamiliar beings... I *had* wanted to grow stronger my own way, but I was growing tired of all this! I needed a break!

I silently thought as much to the god of breasts who dwelled in some other world.

-O●O-

"Yo, Saji," I said, trying to wake my friend, who was lying unconscious in the middle of the battlefield.

He had already reverted to his original form.

"Wha...?! Hyoudou...? The fight?"

It looked like he was awake but still couldn't move his body. I called Asia over and asked her to tend to him.

When Saji was able to sit upright, I informed him, "It's over. A lot happened, but we won."

Saji flashed me a forced smile. "...I see. I don't really remember much of it... But I heard your voice. I was happy. It was so painful. I felt like my whole body was on fire. When I heard you, it felt reassuring."

"Ha-ha-ha. Leave it to me. But don't go on another rampage like that, okay?"

"Seriously? I went on a rampage? Me?"

"Yeah, completely berserk. Still, it's why we won. Your support technique was amazing."

Hearing this, Saji looked relieved. "…I suppose that's all right, then. However…"

Saji glanced around at the aftermath. The abandoned quarry was in ruins. There were craters everywhere that clearly hadn't been there before. It looked like a war zone.

Everyone else was overjoyed at our victory. Xenovia and Irina looked exhausted and were sitting together on the ground.

Team Vali was nowhere to be seen. They had left before any of us noticed, which was typical of them. Vali hadn't returned, either… Had he won? I didn't think he was dead, and yet…

With the overwhelmed Loki held captive, Rossweisse made sure to bind him several times over with some sort of Norse magic.

The Mjölnir hammer may have been a replica, but even so, it had been inordinately powerful. I'd boosted that strength several times over, but in the end, it *had* defeated a god.

"Stuff like this is becoming pretty standard for you, huh? Fighting gods, Demon Kings, Heavenly Dragons, you name it," Saji said with admiration.

"Well, the Gremory Familia has been through a lot. I've heard some people say that they're drawn to the powers of the Red Dragon Emperor. But seriously, I've been so close to death more times than I can count now."

It had basically been constant life-and-death struggles ever since I had become a demon. How had I wound up facing one legendary being after another? No matter how many lives I had, they would run out eventually…

"That's what I mean. You're amazing. I was so scared when Azazel sent me to do that special training. I couldn't stop shaking, and all I wanted was to go home. Yet if I ran away, I'd never have been able to show my face to the chairwoman or the others again…"

"I'm in a similar situation. Honestly, I'm terrified most of the time, but I don't have any other choice. I have to keep going. It looks like the road to becoming a harem king will be a bumpy one, so all I can do is push through every obstacle that gets in my way. Making my dreams come true and protecting what's dear to me means I need to learn how to make full use of everything the Red Dragon Emperor can offer, no matter what."

Saji flashed me a rueful grin. "...I'm no match for you. You lecherous pervert."

Wearing a beautiful smile, Asia declared, "All healed!"

Saji, it seemed, was back to normal.

"Asia, see to the others first. You can leave me for last," I said to her.

Reluctantly, she accepted. "...All right. I understand. But don't do anything silly. Make sure to get some rest." Then she hurried over to the others.

"Issei." The prez was calling for me, but she was staring at Akeno.

Akeno was trying to help Baraqiel to his feet. Asia had already healed his physical wounds, but he must have exhausted himself fighting. His injuries were closed, but he'd lost a lot of blood.

Baraqiel's burly frame was too much for his daughter to support on her own. I understood intuitively what the prez was trying to tell me.

I'm on it!

I rushed to join Akeno and Baraqiel, silently lending a shoulder to the fallen angel.

"...Br—no, Issei Hyoudou."

Baraqiel looked surprised that I would aid him.

He had definitely been about to call me Breast Dragon Emperor, but I didn't really mind.

"Just so you know, I don't feed off breasts," I stated with a wry grin.

"A-ah. Right."

Perhaps it was my imagination, but Baraqiel looked embarrassed. I guess even a stoic guy like him could blush every now and then.

"M-my daughter...Akeno. Do you care for her?" the weakened fallen angel asked.

"Yes. I love her. She's trustworthy and kind," I answered without hesitation.

It looked like Baraqiel was pleased to hear my reply, but it was hard to know for certain.

Akeno, still beneath her father's other arm, turned red.

Faced with such a cute reaction, *I* would probably end up blushing before long.

"...I see," Baraqiel muttered, his voice sounding surprisingly content.

We helped him to a transportation circle and sent him to rejoin his allies, who had been offering logistical support remotely.

"Now then, Issei Hyoudou. You can still move, I assume? It's time to clean up this mess. We need to restore this whole area," Tannin said, recruiting me into assisting him with this thankless task.

And so I worked until dawn trying to fill all the craters Vali had left littered across the quarry.

Dammit! Valiiiii! Where did you go?!

Surveillant

"So those two were the Red Dragon Emperor and the White Dragon Emperor? And we've confirmed the presence of Vritra and the Holy King Sword. Vritra entered a burst state, although it was achieved via a heretofore-unseen approach. And as our information suggested, the Holy King Sword is irregular as well."

"We were right to observe them. This seems to confirm the technology department's theory—that Sacred Gear hosts who come into contact with either the Red or White Dragon Emperor have a high likelihood of undergoing an irregular awakening."

"That Grigori technology also poses a threat... Have you found a way to overcome their Juggernaut Drives?"

"I believe we may be able to counter them by using a Sacred Gear that accelerates the rate of the target's energy consumption. We could use it to exhaust their demonic powers or their life force. The problem is the Red Dragon Emperor. Based on our information, he labors to develop an alternate method of accessing his Juggernaut Drive.

He may be trying to delve into the submerged consciousnesses of the Longinus. The White Dragon Emperor could attempt something similar before long as well."

"...I've just received a message from Cao Cao. Ah, I see..."

"What is it? Don't tell me—"

"Yes, we've located the Dragon Eater. With this, we can bring an end to their so-called *infinity*."

Vali Lucifer

"I may not have used it for a while, but I managed to weather my Juggernaut Drive. All the same, I would like to limit how many times I have to use it, if possible. I'll burn myself out at this rate... How did things go on your end, Arthur?"

"We may be able to manage Fenrir with the master Excalibur... However, the bonds will considerably limit his total strength... I can understand your interest in that creature's fangs, but you certainly have some odd ideas. I'd never let such a dangerous beast join our ranks."

"Vali, we've got word from Cao Cao."

"What does he want now, Bikou?"

"Basically, he's saying they're going it alone. And telling us not to get in their way."

"Cao Cao... Let us pray we don't meet again. We won't hold back if you come after us."

"That Issei Hyoudou sure is a blast, huh? Who would've guessed he'd get a god from another world to cover his back? At the rate he's growing, he'll smash all the records faster than you can say 'go'!"

"Heh. Breast Dragon? For such an absurd title, it won't be long before he's no laughing matter."

Boss×Boss

"I'm sorry I can't say this in person, but it seems you're responsible for saving my family again, Azazel."

"Don't worry about it. But you know, Sirzechs, it was a rough ride this time."

"It also sounds like our Breast Dragon saved the day again."

"Yep, that Issei is just brimming with weird powers. Just who was that god of breasts supposed to be...?! And are you sure it's all right not to mention that other matter to him?"

"You're referring to his promotion, I assume?"

"Issei's, Kiba's, and Akeno's names were all brought up."

"Indeed. We've weathered Kokabiel's attack, the terrorist assault during the peace conference between the three great powers, and the one on the day of the party that the other Demon Kings and I held in the underworld. Most recently, there was that trouble with the old demon regime. Every one of them was a major issue, and each time, Rias and her Familia stepped up to stop the threat. They've earned their promotions and then some. And now they've aided in Loki's capture. Their advancement is all but guaranteed."

"Well, their accomplishments are top of the class, especially given how accustomed to peace most other demons have become. Issei is especially popular in the underworld as the Red Dragon Emperor. Akeno is Baraqiel's daughter. And Kiba can generate irregular Holy Demon Swords. They're all distinguished, promising individuals. As far as power is concerned, they're already at the level of high-class demons. And yet..."

"Yeah, it's still too soon. Issei, in particular, has only been a demon for the past six months. If we promote him immediately, it'll draw our enemies' eyes. Personally, I'd like him to develop his strength more before he's moved up a rank. I think he needs to wait for five, actually, make it three years. Unfortunately, public opinion is pushing for it to be now."

"Ha-ha-ha, it must be hard being a Demon King! So what are your overall feelings, then?"

"There's no question that he deserves a promotion. He will need to carry a title of some kind if he is to continue my lineage with my sister and her Familia, however. The old demon families are very particular on that. But not only is he still too young, but it's also still too soon. I would like him to remain the Breast Dragon for a while yet."

"That makes sense. We should probably keep observing his progress, then… Still, I don't think we're going to have to wait long."

"Yes, I suspect not."

"Issei has his sights set on becoming a harem king, and he's working to pull off one achievement after another to make that dream a reality. Although, when he's promoted—"

"The question is what he will do from there. That will be his true debut as a demon."

"And then there's the issue of the Hero Faction."

"Have you learned anything?"

"The Sacred Gear hosts who we captured have all met unnatural deaths."

"…All of them?"

"Yeah. Ophis's serpents seem to be the cause."

"So we were right. They all took them."

"No, these ones are different. The hosts themselves didn't consume them… This new type coils around a Sacred Gear. From what we've discerned, they're designed to stimulate the Sacred Gears themselves. In all likelihood, they function to forcefully maximize the potential not of their human hosts, but of the Sacred Gears and their innate powers. The end result isn't a boosted attack power. Instead, it's a trigger to unlock one's Balance Breaker. Naturally, it's a delicate and dangerous process. If there's even a tiny slipup, the Sacred Gear is eradicated. Even so, they've been running these experiments practically nonstop. I tried examining the leftover serpents, but they've been designed to stop functioning once their host dies or unlocks their Balance Breaker. It's a brutal tactic, but their Balance Breakers will outnumber ours significantly if it continues."

"…So this is all to add more Balance Breaker users to their ranks? If a Sacred Gear breaks, its user dies, too. I can't believe they truly don't mind sacrificing their own people if it means unlocking a few extra Balance Breakers…"

"The sudden influx of new Balance Breakers is worrisome enough on its own, but what we need to be most wary of…is the birth of an unknown Longinus."

"…*This is going to get messy. We'll need to take countermeasures against Sacred Gears. Now that you mention it, the most troublesome enemies will be those with unique, aberrant abilities.*"

"If all we were talking about were simple power-ups, it wouldn't be too much of a problem. There are a lot of techniques that can easily suppress Power-type fighters. Sacred Gears might make for interesting research, but they're capable of terrifying feats…"

"*God's parting gift, I suppose you could call them. We've been relying on them for a while without pushing them any further than their base potential, but this…may prove to be a mighty obstacle…*"

New Life

"Ah, the school trip is coming up soon."

I was lazing around the clubroom, preoccupied with thoughts of the upcoming trip.

Old man Odin's talks with the Japanese gods had safely concluded, and he had since returned home. It sounded like they had been a resounding success. I had returned that replica hammer to him as well.

As for Vali... He had wholly vanished, taking Fenrir with him. That was actually a major problem, but seeing as we had captured Loki, we would soon learn everything we needed to know about that oversized wolf and would be able to develop new strategies if we had to face him again.

That White Dragon bastard's real goal had been to capture Fenrir. It was partly our fault for not realizing it, but still, I couldn't forgive him. Just what was he planning to do with that creature?

I guess I had been right all along—I would never see eye to eye with Vali.

Azazel wasn't joining us today.

He had said he was going to see Baraqiel off now that his job here was complete. We had offered to come along, but Azazel had insisted on going alone.

"Issei. We've been busy lately, but we really need to go shopping for things before the school trip," Asia said as she read the pages she had bookmarked in her guidebook.

"Asia, I heard that the school trip is a good chance to wear fancy underwear," Xenovia stated.

Asia's face turned red. "R-really...?"

"Yep. Apparently, if you don't, everyone will laugh at you when we all take a communal bath together or go to a hot spring. I don't have any cute underwear, so maybe we could go shopping together?"

"I—I didn't know the school trip was so involved...!"

That sounded like Kiryuu's doing. Well, from a girl's perspective, a lot of thought probably went into assessing the pros and cons of each piece of underwear. Female society sure sounded strict!

"White is best! That's the primordial style, the kind that would make the Lord and Archangel Michael sigh with satisfaction!" Irina declared enthusiastically.

"Nah, Asia and I are going to wear *lucky* panties!"

"Huh?! M-me too?"

"You can't! The color of the faith is white! Or something embroidered with the cross!"

Our Church Maiden Trio was now arguing over underwear... What the heck had happened to them?

Admittedly, it was kind of peaceful, in its own way. The recent battle now felt very distant.

At that moment, I had a thought.

The stronger we all became, the more we realized that there were greater enemies out there. And for whatever reason, they frequently had it in for us.

It wasn't like I wanted to be the strongest person in the world or anything. Although, I *did* aspire to be the mightiest of Pawns...

That said, if anyone were to attack us here, we needed to be strong enough to drive them off. It was essential for a Familia to fight effectively as a unit.

I myself had to get more powerful, too. I wanted to keep exploring the possibilities Azazel had suggested, to improve myself as the Red Dragon Emperor. The only way that was going to happen was talking some sense into those lingering memories of my predecessors in my Sacred Gear.

Hmm.

I *did* want to develop a new technique. Perhaps I'd ask Azazel for guidance. I could get Kiba and Saji to help, too.

"I'm finished!" came a frantic woman's voice from the center of the clubroom.

It belonged to the silver-haired Valkyrie, Rossweisse, who was weeping uncontrollably.

"Ughhhhh! How cruel! How cruel, Lord Odin! How could you leave me behind?!"

Yep. Odin had gone home without her, just like that. He must have realized by now that she wasn't with him, and yet we had heard nothing...

If he hadn't reached out to her, or any of us for that matter, that could only mean...

"I've been fired! That's what this is! I worked so hard for him, and he left me here in Japan by myself! I mean, I'm incompetent! I can't do my job properly! And I'm a virgin! I've been without a boyfriend for my entire life!"

Rossweisse was falling into the pit of despair.

"Come on, don't cry, Rossweisse. I've made sure there's a job for you here at the academy," the prez encouraged, resting a hand on her shoulder.

"...*Sob.* R-really?"

"Yes. Just like you wanted. A teacher, not a student, right?"

"That's correct... I managed to skip a few grades back home, so I've already completed my studies. I'm young, but I know how to teach."

Seriously? She didn't look much older than the rest of us, and she had already chosen the path of a teacher?

"B-but will I be able to survive in this strange country...? If I go home, everyone will get angry at me... *How dare you come back here without Lord Odin*, they'll say! And then they'll fire me again...! Ugh... And I thought I had finally found a job that would give me a comfortable life!"

She seemed pretty depressed about all this. Returning home without the god she was supposed to protect did sound like trouble, though.

"Hee-hee. Don't worry. I have a plan." The prez approached Rossweisse, showing her a handful of documents. "If you join us in the underworld, you can access all these privileges and benefits."

Rossweisse gasped as she read over the papers. "Impossible! Look at all these insurance benefits... And these are fixed-term payments?!"

"That's right. Quite the bargain, don't you think?"

"They're amazing! I—I never knew demons received all this...! And the base salary is so high! These conditions are much better than over in Valhalla!"

Rias was trying to bribe a Valkyrie!

The prez was acting just like an insurance salesman... This was the epitome of a demon whispering in your ear! Demons made their living by making deals with greedy individuals, after all. And this was a high-level demon putting her mastery to work! The prez had a natural talent for this. She truly was a being of the underworld!

"By the way, you can also get these benefits by joining me."

"...I—I *did* hear that one of the prestigious Demon Kings is a Gremory. Oh, and that certain special products made in the Gremory territory have been selling very well."

"That's right. Such a career path would be at your disposal, should you desire it. We Gremorys are always looking to recruit talented individuals like yourself."

As she continued to tempt poor Rossweisse, the prez pulled something out from her pocket—a crimson chess piece!

"What do you think about joining my Familia and trying some underworld work? With your skills, a Rook piece would allow you to become an armored magic user. All you would need to do is accept this one piece."

Every last one of us in the room was stunned by the prez's offer! How could we not have been?!

That was Rias's final Evil Piece! Her last Rook! She was going to use it to recruit a Valkyrie into our ranks, one with a mastery of spells, no less! At present, the only Wizard-types adept in magic we had were the prez and Akeno, so I understood the logic behind the offer.

Rossweisse becoming a Rook would make her a mobile turret capable of unleashing all manner of spell barrages! Her other techniques were excellent. Honestly, the combination of magic and rook seemed fantastic! I could see it working to everyone's advantage!

On top of that, Rossweisse was a cool beauty and incredibly cute! She had her clumsy moments, too, however...

"...This feels like fate. I may be letting myself get carried away here, but it feels like this was inevitable ever since I first met you in that underworld hospital."

Rossweisse accepted the crimson-colored Evil Piece. As she did so, a bright red glow filled the room—and demon wings sprouted from her back.

All it had taken was one Rook piece. Given that she was a Valkyrie, a Norse battle maiden, I had wondered whether one would be enough. Maybe Norse people had a different kind of affinity with Evil Pieces?

"It was recently announced that unused Evil Pieces would grow in response to the demon who owns them," Kiba explained to me. "The Demon King Ajuka Beelzebub, who first made the system, is famous for hiding unused features like that in his programming."

If I understood it right, there were yet unknown elements to the Evil Pieces system.

And demon society was equally impressive for allowing that kind of thing. Maybe they liked adding a little irregularity here and there? I did seem to remember them getting more excited whenever a Rating Game match took an unexpected turn. There was a lot of variation when it came to reincarnated demons, too, so there were a great many possibilities available.

The silver-haired Rossweisse bowed to each of us. "Everyone, I'm Rossweisse, a former Valkyrie, and I've just been reincarnated as a demon. The pension and healthcare plans in the underworld seem to be much better than in my homeland, and I was offered a high degree of financial and job security, so I've decided to enter your ranks. I look forward to working with you all."

Her expression gave off a kind of brainwashed vibe...

"You heard it, everyone. Rossweisse is the Gremory Familia's second Rook," the prez stated with a smile.

She truly was an expert at manipulating others' greed—a genuine demon!

"Well, I guess that's fine. I joined out of desperation, too," Xenovia remarked as she sipped at her tea.

I couldn't deny that there *was* some similarity in how the two of them had been added to our Familia.

"*Welcome!*" we greeted in unison.

We were all happy to have Rossweisse, of course. And how could I say no? Another beautiful woman joining our Familia? Count me in!

First Xenovia and now Rossweisse. The prez had used up her remaining pieces rather quickly.

"Oh-ho-ho-ho-ho-ho! When next we meet, Lord Odin, you'll be in for a reckoning!" Rossweisse muttered with a creepy smile.

She was so scary! A powerful aura was emanating from her! It looked like she genuinely resented the old geezer! Maybe Rossweisse wasn't entirely all right in the head...

For better or for worse, our Familia was now complete.

There was the prez, Akeno, Kiba, Asia, Koneko, Xenovia, Gasper, Rossweisse, and me. Nine of us in total.

We would have to think of some new battle formations.

Just as I was pondering potential strategies, Akeno handed me a bento box.

"This is extra, but you can have it if you like, Issei."

Stewed meat and potatoes?

I picked up a piece in my fingers and lifted it to my mouth. The taste of a wonderful seasoning spread across my tongue.

"...It's delicious, Akeno! I don't really know how to describe it, but it makes my heart feel at ease! It's different to how my mom makes it, but it still tastes like home cooking!"

Akeno handed me a pair of chopsticks, and I began to dig in. You've just gotta trust me, it seriously was delicious!

Akeno joyfully smiled as I devoured the food.

"I'm so glad you're enjoying it... Oh, your lips."

Wondering if I had food stuck to my face, I lifted my hand to brush if off. Before I could, Akeno's face drew close—

Kiss.

For a brief second, her lips pressed against my own.

...

It had been the lightest of brushes, but...it had definitely been...

"Oh-ho-ho. That's my first kiss, you know?" Akeno said, her cheeks tinged red.

A k-k-kiss?!

Did that even count?! It hadn't been intense, that was for sure, but our mouths had most certainly made contact!

The other girls had been watching this whole time and were now fixing me with murderous glares!

"Issei?"

"...Issei?"

"Care to explain yourself?"

"Issei?"

The prez, Koneko, Xenovia, and Asia all approached me, each of them absolutely terrifying!

Why does this always have to happen to meeeee?! I cried internally, to no avail.

"Kiba, Gasper, heeeeelp!"

The male members of this Familia had sworn back when we were training to always come to one another's aid!

However, Kiba merely shrugged, flashing me a forced smile, while Gasper literally ran away and hid in his cardboard box! Did our manly promise to have each other's backs mean nothing?!

Gah!

Akeno wrapped her arms around me from behind as the prez and the others moved nearer! She seemed so happy! And there, right in front of everyone, she declared, "I love you, Issei. Oh-ho-ho."

The prez positively fumed upon hearing this, her crimson aura flaring dangerously!

"Ngh! Issei! Akeno! I'll never forgive you for this!"

Thus did my daily life grow more hectic…

Papa

Now that the trouble with Loki was over, I—Azazel—had joined Baraqiel to go shopping for souvenirs.

It sounded like a bunch of those idiots down in headquarters had asked him to bring some keepsakes back with him from the human realm. They were always putting in obnoxious requests like this. Well, with me as their governor, maybe that couldn't be helped.

I was taking a break on a bench in the department store when Baraqiel returned, his hands filled with shopping bags.

"…Hmm. This should be everything they asked for."

"Good work."

He sat down beside me, looking exhausted. Seeing how stiff-laced Baraqiel was, this sort of activity couldn't have been easy for him. But whenever he was entrusted with a task, he was the kind of person who saw it through to the very end.

I pulled a bento box from my drawstring bag, handing it to him. "Here, take it, Baraqiel."

"What's this?" he asked.

"Just open it," I urged him.

"…A boxed lunch?"

Akeno had asked me to deliver it to Baraqiel earlier. Truthfully, she'd given no verbal instruction, but it was apparent who the food was meant for.

"This…" When Baraqiel opened the box, we saw a wide assortment of multicolored Japanese-style foods packed inside.

Baraqiel glanced across at me. Suppressing a grin, I urged him to dig in.

He picked up his chopsticks and started by bringing a piece of potato to his mouth.

At that moment…a tear ran down his cheek.

"…Stewed meat and potatoes… Just like how Shuri used to make them…"

He began to shovel one item into his mouth after the next, his chopsticks moving in swift silence.

The man was completely absorbed in the food, tears streaming from his eyes.

I glanced over at my close friend. "Let me, Rias, and the others look after Akeno. Everything's fine. The man she's fallen for may be a bit of an idiot, and a pervert, too, but he's a good guy."

Baraqiel stopped eating for a second, covering his eyes with his hand. Muffling a sob, he said to me, "I…want to believe…that he'll take good care of her…"

"You've got nothing to worry about there."

"H-he doesn't feed off women's breasts?"

"Nope."

"I see…"

Baraqiel let out a sigh of relief before returning his attention to the food.

That cooking of the woman he loved, something he thought he would never taste again, had found its way back to him after all this time.

And you'll be able to eat more of it, buddy, as much as you want. And, Issei…I could never say this to your face…but I think I owe you one.

"Dammit. I'd never have thought I'd meet a dragon who can make people happy through breasts."

Heroes

"It won't be long before they realize what we're up to, Cao Cao."

"Yes, they're drawing close. But that's fine. We've amassed enough in the way of new recruits. Perhaps we should proceed to the next stage?"

"Indeed. We're almost ready. It's time."

"In that case, who should we negotiate with first?"

"Do you think they'll fall for it? Stripping away their alliances one by one, I mean."

"Oh, they will. No one wants a full-scale war in this day and age. That was why the old demon regime failed. First, we open negotiations. Everything will proceed as planned, Siegfried."

"Understood. The only ones capable of defeating Demon Kings, monsters, and dragons alike—"

"Are heroes. As it has ever been."

AFTERWORD

Next time you're at that famous underworld hamburger chain McDemon's, order yourself a kids' meal, and you'll get a limited-edition Breast Dragon or Switch Princess figurine! Collect both and make the Breast Dragon power up! Don't delay, children! Make your way to McDemon's while supplies last!

Hi there. Ishibumi here. The tale of the Breast Dragon Emperor has reached its seventh volume and entered a new chapter!

The final member of Rias's Familia has been revealed—the former Valkyrie, Rossweisse! She showed up briefly in Volume 5, but now she's become a full cast member. She might seem cool and reserved from the outside, but she also has a certain unhealthy, perverse side to her. I hope you're all excited to meet her!

Rossweisse is a Wizard-type fighter, but she also leans toward the Technique side of the spectrum. With her, Rias has gained a Rook capable of wielding Norse magic, a mobile cannon of sorts. The Gremory Familia really is a force to be reckoned with.

In terms of age, she's around seventeen or eighteen. Also, she isn't a student at Kuou Academy, but an instructor. Of course, she will be accompanying Issei and the gang on the school trip. Say hello to Ms. Rossweisse!

After the incident in the last volume, Issei and Asia have found themselves in a more lovey-dovey relationship. Akeno was the main heroine this time around, so we didn't get to see a whole lot of Issei and Asia together, but rest assured that they are doting on each other at school and at home. Behind the scenes, Issei is also busy getting close to Rias… The two of them sure make for a cloyingly sweet couple, don't you think?

As we enter a new arc in the series, Issei's growth will similarly enter a new phase. We only saw him standing at the entrance to it in this book. Will he be able to lift the curse of the Red Dragon Emperor? He'll need to find a more unique way of powering up—one that is different from his Juggernaut Drive. Do watch over him as he keeps pressing forward in this new arc.

The god of breasts is kind of like an Easter egg that only rarely reveals itself to Issei, so please don't take it too seriously.

Now, on to the other characters.

It's a delicate time for the Two Heavenly Dragons. Ddraig and Albion were both reduced to tears this volume. Strictly speaking, that was all Issei's fault… Those poor dragons. Please, dear reader, lend them your support. They aren't at all wicked creatures!

And then we have pitiable dragon number three, Tannin. Again, it's because of Issei that he was reduced to a comedic role. Issei seems to think he can ask the former Dragon King for anything when he's in trouble! And this time, he went all out in battle. Issei is lucky to have such an encouraging master.

The soul of Vritra was reawakened inside Saji during his earlier battle with Issei, and so Saji appeared at the tail end of this volume as a creature of black flame. He still hasn't mastered those powers, so who knows what additional abilities he'll uncover? He might develop in a completely different direction from Issei.

Lastly, we have Asia. The battle this time around would have been perilous without her healing ability. That skill has become indispensable to the Gremory Familia, wouldn't you say? And the other members all understand that they need to protect her with their lives… Yes, she has been growing, too…

*   *   *

We can't forget about the Khaos Brigade.

The Hero Faction has been up to no good, operating in the shadows. Just what are they hoping to accomplish with all those Sacred Gear hosts? They're definitely planning something different from what the old demon regime wanted. Rest assured, they will begin to play an even larger role in the story come Volume 8.

Vali and his team have gone rogue, too. They aren't cooperating with the Hero Faction, and even though they fought alongside Issei and the others this time around, everyone will still have to be on guard against them going forward. The Two Heavenly Dragons are forging a unique relationship and have started acknowledging each other's skills, but just how far will this accord develop?

The next arc will shine a spotlight on the concept of Sacred Gears, which have generally played supporting roles up until now. I think we've been able to catch a good glimpse of just how disturbing and creepy they can be. When an ability we all considered to be nothing more than a convenient power-up is turned against our protagonists, just how much of a threat will it pose?

Lastly, let me offer my thanks.

We've successfully gotten Volume 7 out the door. I'm especially grateful to Miyama-Zero and my editor, H!!

The next volume is all about the school trip! Issei will be actively exploring the old city of Kyoto! Or will he? Did someone say that it's going to be a collection of short stories? We may have to call it Volume 7.5!

We received a lot of requests from readers to compile the short stories featured in *Dragon Magazine* into the next volume. Unlike the main narrative, these works have more of a comedic focus. It's *DxD* from a completely different angle, but Issei and our many heroines are a lot more erotic than they are in the main volumes, so look forward to that! We're also planning to include the beautiful illustrations that Miyama-Zero made for the *Dragon Magazine* versions, but that will depend on how many short stories we can fit in the book! Plus, there's going to be a *yuki-onna*! Everyone involved has been enjoying the short stories just as much as the main narrative, so I hope you will, too! The compilation should be available sometime in the fall.

Okay, time for some quick self-promotion! By the time this seventh volume reaches store shelves, the September issue of *Dragon Magazine* should also be available, and that will include a special booklet with the first part of a manga adaptation of *High School DxD*, illustrated by Hiroji Mishima! Anyone who wants to see more of Rias's breasts should make sure to keep an eye out for it!